"Allan Richard Shickman's Zan-Gah is a terrifically exciting adventure that will appeal to young adults and their elders too. Richly imagined and beautifully written, with characters and settings unlike any I've read, I believe Zan-Gah will be read and reread for many years to come."

— Scott Phillips, best-selling author of *The Ice Harvest* and *Cottonwood*

"Zan-Gah is one of the best books I ever read...a truly gripping book. The characters are so real I feel like I know them. It gets deep into the mind of not only one, but several. I give this book five stars. I could read it over and over."

— Sam L., age 13

"Zan-Gah was very interesting for a girl my age. I would read it again."

— Elaine H., age 15

"I read a lot of books, so I know a good book when I see one. Zan-Gah is full of creativity and suspense. A wonderful book."

— Elan S., age 11

"I am going to ask my teacher to read it to the class."

— Rider S., age 12

"In Zan-Gah, I entered a world that was terrifying, yet beautiful. This book left me where the best novels aways do—wanting more."

— Bonnie M., teacher

"There are parts of Zan-Gah that I keep thinking about even though I read the story several months ago. I imagined it so much that it feels like I saw the movie of it too."

— Jonah H., age 10

"I dreamed about Zan-Gah in the red terrain of the Land of Red Rocks. Zan-Gah really seeped into me."
                                    — Ally B, Jonah's mom,
                                      psychologist

"I felt transported into another time. I could not put Zan-Gah down until I finished it, and I cried at the end. The words are delicious. For ages 11 to 111."
                                    — Patricia G., English teacher

"I read Zan-Gah to a group of students up to age 13. Each and every one of them enjoyed the adventures of this brave boy. What courage and resourcefulness Zan-Gah exhibited to those children."
                                    — Donna H., teacher's aide

"Zan-Gah paints a detailed picture of the three societies in the book. The plotline is well developed."
                                    — Claire N., age 16

"At times, I felt that I was watching the story unfolding rather than simply reading it."
                                    — Hilarie N., Claire's mom,
                                      academic administrator

"I loved reading Zan-Gah! For me the book was more than just an adventure story. I felt like I was witness to an important moment in humanity's history."
                                    — David S., application developer

"It is refreshing to see a book of this quality published for pre-teens and teens. It is age-appropriate in content, but still challenges the intellect of avid readers of this age group. I know several kids who will want to read Zan-Gah"
                                    — Diane P., editor

"I cried at the end."
                                    — Burton S., age 69

ZAN-GAH

A Prehistoric Adventure

BY ALLAN RICHARD SHICKMAN

EARTHSHAKER BOOKS

ZAN-GAH: A PREHISTORIC ADVENTURE
© Copyright 2007 by Allan R. Shickman

ISBN-13: 978-0-9790357-0-8
ISBN-10: 0-9790357-0-8
LCCN: 2006936675

Published in the United States by
Earthshaker Books
P. O. Box 300184
St. Louis, MO 63130

VISIT OUR WEBSITE AT **WWW.EARTHSHAKERBOOKS.COM**

FOR THE KIDS IN THE FAMILY—EVERYWHERE.

CONTENTS

1 THE LION

From a long distance a traveler, or some wild thing, might see within the deep and absolute blackness of night an intense orange light which looked from afar like a glowing coal. If that observer were curious (or hungry, as was often the case), and had the courage to seek a nearer vantage point, he would see a youthful figure seated on a rock staring into a blazing bonfire. The youth, just in his early teens, wore an expression as intense as his fire, which revealed the preoccupation of one engaged both in thought and action. In his hand he held a staff, one end of which he had briefly placed in the hottest part of the fire. He withdrew it for perhaps the tenth time to scrape the scorched end with a sharp rock, gradually shaping the hard, blunt rod into a pointed weapon. And as he worked he meditated on the events of the coming day.

There would be a hunt. A lion had killed a child and it had to be destroyed. Living, it would be a constant threat to the neighboring clans. The elders had put aside their differences in order to unite behind a single strategy in which many would participate. As the sun rose, the males of each tribe would advance toward the wild, uninhabited region which spread between them. The clans did not much like each other, and were glad to have this desolate space separating their campfires—a treacherous, rocky area mostly covered with tall grass and a few trees. It was now known that the beast they sought prowled somewhere within, and their intention was to encircle it. Each hunter would be separated by a considerable distance at first, but gradually they would get closer to each other as they approached their target. A very large circle would get smaller and smaller until the killer lion was sighted somewhere in the middle.

The youth knew what followed. At some point, after the ring of men had tightened around it, the lion would see that it was trapped. At that moment an experienced and watchful leader would give a loud signal to charge, and every man at once would run at it with his spear. They would assail it and harry it as many wolves in a pack combine to attack an animal larger than themselves, striking and worrying and distracting until it was bled, exhausted, and unable to resist its final end.

This was a common method of killing animals, but usually it was used to trap edible game—deer, pigs, and even rabbits. But this would be no rabbit. The lion was the fiercest and most dangerous creature his people ever encountered; and they encountered it by accident and bad luck only. It was avoided as much as anything alive—never sought out except in the utmost necessity. But now they had no choice. It must be killed.

These were the thoughts that absorbed the youngster, and it was for this very hunt that he was sharpening his spear. Although he stared into the fire as if it alone interested him, as if he were hypnotized into rigidity by its flames and sparks, it was the events of the next day that completely held his mind. He took the spear from the fire and blew on the glowing end; and as he did, his face was illuminated for a moment with an eerie light. Scraping it again for the last time, he felt the still hot point with his finger, set it aside, and looked once more into the fire.

It was horrible to think about. He knew poor Rias, the boy who had been killed. A little child, he thought, torn to pieces by a savage, hungry animal. In his mind he saw everything in terrible detail. His lip trembled, and he felt an unwelcome sickness of fear which he resisted with all of his strength. He lifted the spear yet again and honed it mechanically as he sought to steel himself for the coming day. He was afraid with all his heart, but he also knew that he must conquer his fear; because in moments of great danger, to be afraid is the surest way to die. It was not just a matter of preparing a weapon. Above all, he must prepare himself. The danger not only crouched out there in the wilderness; it crouched inside as well.

Although the lad by the fire wore the skin of an animal, he was not comfortably warm. One side of his body was too hot while the other was like ice. He changed his position, turning his face to the blackness and peering into its depths. His thoughts of the lion were brought from the coming day to the present moment. Might it not be nearer than he supposed, stalking him and watching his every move? He looked and listened intently to the tiny noises of the night. There was no danger—at least no more than usual. Animals feared fire. That was one of the few powerful advantages people had over them. He piled the fire high with twigs and coarser wood and welcomed the crackling response. Then he stabbed the spear into the flank of an imaginary animal, and with a ruthless expression wrenched it from the wound. Tomorrow, in the hunt, he would stand his ground, but now it was time to lie down.

Gripping his newly fashioned weapon, he stepped into the opening of the cave where several families lay asleep. They were all huddled together almost upon one another for warmth, still clinging to their spears and weapons. Their long-drawn breath froze as they exhaled. He lay down next to his mother and felt the warmth of her body. She jerked to feel the iciness of his, grunted, and went back to sleep. In time he too was asleep, breathing heavily.

The youth's name was Zan, which in his tongue meant Hunter. He and his people had a language, but we no longer know it. It was spoken in an era so remote in time that there were as yet no nations upon the earth, no cities, nor written words. Humans lived in caves and hollows or in the crudest man-made shelters—wherever they could establish cover from wind and rain, from wild animals, and from each other. Zan and his kindred lived in that dim period when there was no safety but that supplied by strength and cunning, when there were no laws but those imposed by nature and by humankind's own fierce desire to survive. People faced constant danger, and not many lived to be old.

They were frequently hungry and thirsty. They ate only what they could hunt down or gather in their hands, and had to eat immediately what they could not store. Game was perhaps more plentiful in the summer, but meat kept better during the cold months, and the quarry was easier to see in the winter when there were no sheltering leaves on the trees and tracks could be followed in the snow. Animals also might be weakened by hunger during that season of scarcity, and weakness made them easier to kill. So on the whole, people ate better in the winter, but game was difficult to bring down at any time, and many days could be spent in frozen, fruitless chases. Animals were swifter and often stronger than the men who hunted them, could hear or smell their pursuers from a mile away, and seemed gifted with a special intelligence that humans neither had nor understood. Given these difficulties and rarity of success, it was possible to starve in the midst of relative abundance. When the men did manage to bring down an animal the clan had meat to eat, skins to wear, and horns and bones to fashion into tools—truly a cause for celebration.

Homes and shelters were established where there was a source of water—a lake, river, stream, or spring. Zan's family was lucky, for there was a spring safely within their cave which trickled from its deep, mysterious interior (where only the women were allowed) to the exit and beyond. There also was a river nearby, but the rains had failed for many weeks and it had begun to dry up, so that even the trees flanking it looked parched and sickly.

Zan's people were cold most of the year, but they were as used to it as the animals whose skins they wore. At night Zan slept beneath, and wore each day, the pelt of a goat which his father, Thal, had killed and which his mother, Wumna, had prepared by beating and chewing it until it was soft. Zan was fortunate to have it. Luxury was unknown, and strangers could be envious of a scrap of fur or a bit of food. Tools and weapons, crude as they were, were valued and guarded. A stone blade, which took a week's labor to make, might induce an uncouth ruffian to take a life in order to possess it. It is hard to imagine how much simple things were prized and coveted in that frightful time. Darkness was indeed darker to them then, coldness colder, and the cruelest passions somehow crueler and more deeply passionate.

Winter was approaching, the nights were long, and Zan had a deep if comfortless sleep. The family awoke, first one then another, to the sound of each other's snorts and the chill of the morning air. Zan was the last to stir. Upon rising they saw that their world was gray with mist—a good sign because the tribes had lately been oppressed by drought. For the coming hunt it might be helpful or dangerous. They would not be able to see their fierce quarry, but the lion would not see them either at first. It would only hear the approach and fearful din of many men. By the time the hunters drew near, the fog would have burned away and all would happen as planned—*unless it happened some other way, some unforeseen way.*

Zan's father, Thal, would have been happy to have let him sleep. He had little desire to see a boy so young participate in the hazardous business before them. Zan, eager to assume a manhood not yet his, had raged and demanded the right to join, to carry a spear and raise his cry against the great cat. At last his father had yielded (to the horror of his mother), but warned him to stay close—closer by far than the men would be to each other. He impressed on his son the great peril, thinking in his troubled heart that the boy had to learn to deal with the difficulties of manhood sooner or later. But Zan was not a man, and when he rose that dismal morning the fears of the previous night returned to him and had to be conquered anew. In truth, every man among them shared his feelings to some extent and swallowed them down as he did, none allowing himself to ask whether this dangerous labor might prove to be his last. They made jokes at the beast's expense and at their own, clapping each other on the back or shoulder and uttering gruff words of encouragement. No one spoke of fear.

The appointed time had come. Each hunter grasped a spear, and many took a drum or hollowed log to beat with the end of his weapon. The sun, vaguely visible, was rising over the misty terrain, signaling the first stage of their design. As the males of Zan's clan spread out to form a great arc perhaps three miles long, strong legs carried them toward the great rock, Gah, where they would join the second arc of men. When the five clans finally connected, their circle would be nearly fifteen miles around. Speed was required. Zan struggled to keep up with his father, a powerful runner who urged him on, exhaling heavily as he spoke—with each stride a word or two: "Have courage...boy...courage....The...first...rule...

is...to...always...face...your...enemy." His voice was deep and sure despite his breathlessness, and as he panted his words out, they seemed to freeze as vapor on the morning air. "Better...to...die...than...to...flee...in...the... presence...of...danger....And...more...likely...to...die...if... you...show...your...back....Be brave...be brave...and live!"

The region that the hunters wished to surround was rocky and uneven. Tall grasses grew wherever there was soil to receive them, and there were many places where a crouching lion might hide. Indeed, there was always the possibility that the great cat would escape in between the men who were encircling it, for they were hundreds of paces apart in the beginning. To prevent this, noise would be the first weapon they would use. The hunters would make a great, unaccustomed racket that the beast would avoid; so instead of breaking through their scattered ranks it would head right toward the center of the tightening ring of men. In one way lions were like people. They were frightened by what was unfamiliar. That was what the hunters were counting on as they raised their cries.

All of the five segments came together at about the same time, so it was as if a circle of men had appeared from nowhere. Only Zan stood close to his father, otherwise the distance between each hunter was considerable. It would gradually lessen as they progressed. The mist still obscured their vision but it was beginning to fade. If only the monster would stay away for a short while! If only it would refrain from springing suddenly out of the white vapor to kill before it was even sighted! Something like that had actually occurred a few seasons earlier during a similar hunt, Thal recalled to his son. They had not been looking for a lion but they had found one! On that occasion a man had been badly mauled before the animal could be speared. Zan did not remove his eyes from the direction of danger, and in fact everyone had placed his senses on alert.

Having formed a boundary, they turned toward the center of the great area it encompassed, where the killer lion was believed to lie hidden. Then they started their advance with grim faces and firm, deliberate steps that were at once cautious and determined. Zan followed the footsteps of Thal, wading through dried grass that was up to the waist of the grown men but reached almost to his shoulders. A few men carried torches of pitch or fat. Animals would fear the smell as much as the fire itself, and run from it. Some set the dry grass on fire as well and used it as their ally, carefully noting the direction of the wind.

The beating of logs and drums began. First, a single drum echoed across the plain, answered by another far off, and joined by a great tribal yell that shook the region. A third drum beat, while other men hammered their shields with their spears, each establishing a distinct, powerful rhythm. Another and another entered in, each with his own sound, creating a dense texture of rhythms which charged every man with needed strength and purpose. The drums boomed a vibrant, manly thunder that filled Zan with courage and resolve. It helped him to feel part of a single force, huge and alive. Now, strong men with fiery, determined eyes roared out a cry of battle. A deep-throated chant was hallooed forth, a mixture of songs and cries that would surely appall the lion while encouraging themselves: *Kika kika kak, kika kika kak! Tona hai, tona hai!* Run, monster, run! And their voices, combining with the percussion of their rude instruments, wrought a pitch of noise so fearful that it reached into Zan's very entrails and bewitched the hairs on his head. *Kika kika kak! Kika kak! Tona hai! Tona hai!*

So they proceeded, and before very long someone not far from Zan shrilly cried out: *O ah ah, O ah ah!* The cat had been spotted leaping above the smokey grass and then disappearing into one of the numberless nooks or hiding places. Again from another quarter as the men strode ahead came the eagle cry: *O ah ah, O ah ah!* The hunters did not increase their speed but redoubled their thunderous beats. In unison now they hurled out their songs of courage and attack, and now and again the shriller cry of *O ah ah* informed the hunters of the beast's movements.

Now it was seen by all of the men in Zan's vicinity, running in the opposite direction, and soon turning back again or to the right or left as the hunters closed in. The circle was still very large, making a charge impossible, so the elder gave no signal. Meanwhile, the lion was looking for refuge, not only from the men but from the appalling noise. It was so loud that every hollow of the earth resounded in its ears. The enormous, unaccustomed din pulsed out from all directions was working its potent magic, and might have put a whole herd of savage animals to confusion and flight. This was a creature whose sensitive ears could hear from some distance the smallest movement in the grass. It could not endure the amazing man-made thunder.

The hunters, whose dark bodies were now visible opposite against the rising mist, converged toward a clearing paved with rough stones; and there the beast paced and growled, with little natural cover to hide itself. It was a lioness, a female, and doubly to be feared. She began to move warily in a circle as the men tightened the trap, and as they got closer the lioness began to stride and prowl in a circle so small that she almost seemed to be chasing her tail. But she was watching, watching while she turned and snarled, for a weakness in the ever-tightening ring of her pursuers. Then, at the moment the attack finally was sounded—when the men, putting down their drums and torches, charged on the run with their spears—the lioness saw what she was looking for. One of her enemies was smaller, weaker than the rest. There was a point in the strengthening line that could be broken! Thought merged with furious action and the beast, with a mighty bound of astonishing swiftness, darted toward Zan. Five hundred pounds of snarling fury sprang directly at him with claws bared and fanged mouth open!

In the last instant Zan could see the now bright sun shining into the lion's crimson mouth, and he saw as well his mother, his lost brother, his toys, and his entire childhood race before his eyes. It all happened so suddenly that there was nothing anyone could do. Even his father, who was a little in front but several paces away, could give him no aid. Zan would have to protect himself.

He held his sharp spear, almost twice his height, rigidly before him, pointing it straight at the lion's dreadful face. The beast leapt directly at him, razor claws extended. Quick as fire Zan thrust the point into the oncoming jaws. The weapon never left his hand until it was deep in the animal's throat and coming out the back of its muscular neck.

The lion's own great power and weight were Zan's friends. Possibly the beast, concentrating on the boy rather than what he held in his hand, did not even see the spear. She saw only a weak youth whom she would rend like a rabbit. But in leaping upon him the monster ran into the firmly held weapon. Zan had not even thrown it; all he did was hold it steadily before him. But that was a great deal indeed! Few among the clans, child or man, could have faced a moment of such terrible danger so steadfastly.

The lioness was not dead. She rolled and twisted in anguish, roaring, clawing at the spear in her maw, and wounding the ground with her great paws as she writhed. The warriors of the clans felt no touch of pity. They stood around her, silent and awed, watching the death-agony. None raised another spear to her for they saw that it would not be necessary, and would even be impious—disrespectful to the animal's noble spirit. Nor did they wish to further damage the beautiful and valuable pelt. Then the famous elder of the northern clan took a great rock and threw it onto the dying lion's head. The others followed his example, each throwing a stone (though not such a large one) at the creature that had caused them so much trouble and fear. If you had asked them why one and all bothered to do so, they might have said that it was for luck, but deep in their hearts they wanted to reassure themselves that they, not she, had conquered.

Zan was wounded. The lioness had marked his arms and shoulders with her claws, and dark streaks of blood showed like stripes upon them. They would be seen long after as honorable scars, reminders of the heroic action of this day. People were accustomed to accepting injuries worse than these. One at work might almost cut off a finger by accident and just go on working, muttering to himself. Zan's father was not overly concerned and neither was Zan. These hurts would heal.

What followed was not merely celebration and excitement; it was hysteria, a wild overflow of cheer that attends a difficult conquest—that bursts forth when endangered men overcome great challenge and peril. Zan's kindred gathered around him and he was raised aloft, still bleeding, onto the shoulders of his father and his huge, hairy uncle—men of known strength and honor. From his mighty chest Zan's uncle, Chul, sent forth a cry of triumph which was seconded by Thal and by every man. Their gravel voices vented their exultation with a sound so leaden that heard far off it was like a moan or a lament. The women, who had been left behind when the hunt began, heard it and knew that it was no moan but a signal of success. The lion had been killed. And they too sent up shrill cheers and ululation.

The drums began to clamor again and the hunters sang a deep-throated hymn of manly victory. Zan, still on the shoulders of his kin, was the center of their celebration. He was greeted by all, and clapped on his thighs by their friendly hands. Had the strongest warrior of the tribe brought the great beast down, he would have been honored in the same way; but that it was accomplished, unaided, by a mere boy struck the multitude with wonder, and moved all hearts in his favor.

Now, the great elder of the northern clan came forward, and all were silent. Aniah was his name. Of all the men in the five clans, he was acknowledged as the greatest—an old warrior covered with scars, his white hair flying in the wind. Because he was not of Zan's people, his notice was doubly to be valued, and Zan was filled with pride. Aniah made no speech. He simply struck Zan roughly on the thigh with his sinewy hand and said *"Zan-Gah."* Zan of the Rock! Zan who began his trial of manhood at the great rock, Gah, and who stood like a rock, immovable in the face of overwhelming danger!

The tribes took up the new name as if it were a cry of battle, and with it hallooed their regard. *Zan-Gah! Zan-Gah! Zan-Gah!* It was the raw release of gruff, brute men whose roaring rose from their hearts and stomachs. They bellowed and chanted in ecstasy, dancing and thumping their weapons and hollow drums. *Zan-Gah! Zan-Gah! Zan-Gah! Zan-Gah! Zan-Gah!* and so carried the boy all the way to his cave dwelling where his mother, Wumna, awaited his return with tears of gladness and no little astonishment. Several men had tied the lion's legs to two poles to carry it away on their shoulders. The prized skin would be Zan's.

The heavy carcass was given to the women of the tribe because it was female. Had it been a male, the men would have skinned it themselves and removed its insides, but they were not allowed to violate the secrets of a lioness. It was a matter of respect. Zan was permitted to recover his spear from its mouth, and he had a chance to examine the huge head and jaws. A tremor passed through him as he touched them. The large, dead eyes were still open, and the beast did not respond as he pulled the lips aside to look at the terrible fangs. With a frown he placed his foot on the lion's great muzzle and wrenched the spear, all bloody, from the animal's mouth. He held it aloft and the women resumed their high-pitched ululation.

They rubbed Zan's wounds with an inky substance which would aid the healing, but leave dark marks when the wounds closed. Having earned his scars, Zan had no wish for them to disappear. Then the women hung the animal by its forelegs, cut it open so that its entrails spilled onto the ground, and carefully stripped off the tawny pelt. The body was hewn apart to be roasted, for everybody would want to taste it—not because it was good to eat, but because the eaters hoped and expected to benefit by doing so. A taste of the lion's flesh would give them some of its strength, speed, and ferocity, and it would continue to live in them. That too was a matter of respect.

Deep into the night the celebration continued. The heart of the lion was given to Zan to share with his friends, while the men passed around lion parts and gnawed on the bones. The women joined in too, tasted the flesh, and participated in the dance. Large logs, carved with brute images, were used as pounders, beating out rhythms on the ground to encourage the dance and awaken the spirits of the earth. They sang and chanted old stories of mighty hunters and warriors of the past. They re-enacted the scene of the hunt, showing how Zan had held his spear and stood his ground, wielding their weapons in dance, with every man acting as if he himself had struck the fatal blow. Imitating the lioness too, they play-acted her ferocity and re-enacted her death-throes. Some even lifted a spear to their own mouths to show how it had entered and how the lion had howled and rolled in agony. All rejoiced until they were exhausted. Then, one by one bidding Zan farewell with gestures of regard, they went to their rude homes and frozen beds.

Zan was left alone at last, staring deeply into the waning fire and thinking on the day's events. Now, with the sounds of applause and congratulation dying in his ears, something strange happened. Suddenly he was convulsed by a shudder of fear as real as if the terrible beast had reappeared alive before him. He was shaking uncontrollably. His breath left him and his heart started to pound audibly in his chest. He told his body to stop but it would not obey. It just shook more until his teeth chattered. This would pass. Zan knew what was happening. All of his fears had returned to take revenge on him because he had dared that day to stand up to them.

2 THE TWINS

Zan was not handsome. He squinted as if he were constantly watching for something on the horizon, and only at times did his narrowed eyes open wide in happiness or surprise—upon seeing a large hill of ants, a slithering snake, or the unexpected hop of a tiny toad. If he saw a friend approaching he would smile, but he might have smiled more often than he did. His strong white teeth would lighten up his dark face, and it was as if the entire landscape had brightened. Then suddenly the sunny smile would vanish and the grimace would come out of its hiding place—and he would be watching the horizon again.

He was a little short for his age. Other boys no older than he were as much as a head taller, but his body was as hard and wiry as theirs, and had no fat on it. Zan could throw a spear or a rock as well as his friends, and could beat them at wrestling despite their greater size because he was fast, and he knew when and where to use his strength. Zan's impressive scars also made up some for his height, and he had a great bush of curls crowning his head, which made him seem taller than he was. Some day he might lose most of his wild hair as his father and uncle had, and be as bald as they. By then he hoped he would be taller, though he would never be as big as his father, much less his gigantic uncle, Chul.

Although small, Zan had acquired a new sense of sureness since he had killed the lion, a confidence that was seen in his bearing and confirmed by the double name everyone gave him, Zan-Gah. His father now treated him more as an equal. In fact Thal sometimes sought his opinion on matters as well as giving his own, so that the two, father and son, almost became friends. As the season moved toward spring, they hunted and worked together more than ever before, and Thal carefully taught him the skills that he had.

Zan had a twin. Born an hour after Zan, Dael looked exactly like him, and yet in time everybody had been able to tell them apart by their marked differences in character. Zan was serious and talked little, while Dael loved to talk and chatter. Dael was an affectionate child, his arm always around his brother or his father, but Zan was reserved and intense, lacking his twin's happy optimism, and looking inward as much as outward. Smiles visited Zan but seldom while Dael rarely frowned. Although only an hour apart, Zan was like an older brother, stoutly protective of his milder twin.

They were inseparable. Whether hunting or spearing fish, playing or working or climbing a tree to gather the topmost fruit, they were rarely apart. When they were separated even for a few minutes they missed each other. They raced and wrestled like puppies during the day, and slept side by side at night. Dael would tease and joke while Zan mostly listened and sometimes laughed in spite of himself. Once Zan almost fell out of a tree laughing at something his brother said, startling Dael into seriousness. If they played tag, Dael could never catch Zan, but seemed not to care. He was proud of his brother, recognized his physical superiority, and tried to tease Zan's seriousness away. Zan loved and respected Dael for his warm and unique nature, considering him not only his twin but almost his better self.

It was hard to think of them apart. As they roamed or played, their two figures were recognizable from a distance, curls springing like snakes from their heads to form two round globes—seldom one alone. People could never meet with one without asking where the other was, and they were hardly ever spoken of separately.

Then one day Dael disappeared—no one knew where. That had been about a year before. Zan and he had argued over a piece of meat (unworthy quarrel) and Dael had stalked off by himself. That was how they punished each other on the rare occasions that they quarreled, for each knew that the other would miss him, so infrequently were they apart. Zan saw him going and knew that he was angry, but he sullenly took up the stone blade he had been working on and chipped at it with another rock, refusing to speak or even look up until Dael was gone. A while after, he felt some remorse at his stinginess and for letting his brother depart without a word. Dael so seldom asked him for anything, and always shared whatever he had with careless generosity. Awaiting his return, Zan began to wonder that his brother, who never nourished his anger for long, could be so long away. Night came and their parents began to be concerned. When the moon was high overhead Thal, seriously alarmed, left his fire to seek him, spear in hand. Thal was gone for two nights and a morning. He came back alone. He had visited each of the five clans without any luck. Now he returned discouraged, famished (for none had offered him food), and full of care.

Wumna's tearful face was twisted with fear and grief. Wild animals were everywhere, and marauding warriors too—ferocious and savage men, strange in their ways— were known to carry off people to be their slaves, or even to take them for food. She shook her husband desperately for any bit of good news, but his grim and troubled face told her that he had none.

No body was found. A year afterwards, when the remains of young Rias were discovered, it was supposed that the same lioness had pounced on Dael too, but before that no one had known of the beast's existence. Dael's disappearance had been at that time a painful mystery, and in truth it still was. The mangled corpse of poor Rias had been brought home, but nothing of Dael or his possessions. A larger search was begun, enlisting the less than eager aid of the other clans, but although they looked far and wide for a month, Dael was not to be traced.

Dael's mother was crushed with sorrow. She would walk listlessly around the cave dwelling speaking to no one, and looking up suddenly at any sound of approach. Thal, also shaken with grief, watched her and said nothing. Later, when Zan had taken part in the lion hunt,

Wumna was in an agony of fear. She had not gotten over her terrible loss—as if she ever could! A whole year later, she still started when she heard anyone coming, and she became unhealthily protective of her remaining son, wearing a look of sore anxiety whenever he went away even a short distance, and embracing him passionately when he returned.

Zan secretly blamed himself for Dael's disappearance. His grief struck him, not all at once, but little by little until it was a great weight on his heart. Dael was truly gone, and it seemed that Zan, like his mother, would never again be happy. It was as if an important part of himself were lost and he did not know where to look for it. Like Wumna he turned toward the sound of footsteps in hopeful expectation. Sometimes the brush of rustling leaves was enough to arrest his attention and make him look around, ready to rise in joy to receive someone— who was not there. Zan longed to share the story of the lion hunt with his brother—to show him the beautiful pelt and the spear still dark with blood. Dael did not yet know how staunchly he had faced the lioness, nor had he seen the scars of honor that were a record of Zan's bravery. He longed to tell Dael his new name, Zan-Gah, and how the great northern elder had given it to him. But mostly he wished he could throw his arm around Dael's shoulder and tell him that he was sorry.

Zan began to have bad dreams. Some nights he dreamed of the lion and sometimes of his twin—or both. More than once the lion was chasing Dael, and Zan was somehow unable to help because he could not find his spear—and Zan would awaken with his body shaking and his heart pounding as it had the night of the lion hunt. Or Dael would appear to Zan laughing and inviting him to play. Zan, overjoyed to see him, would start to tell Dael about his adventure, only to have the very same lion spring suddenly out of the tall grass and come between them. He often dreamed that he was looking for Dael, but all he ever found was the lioness he sought to avoid. One time, searching where his mother pointed, he found the animal dead and swarming with flies—and for some reason he felt overwhelming pity for it. Then Zan dreamed that Dael, smirking as though he had just played one of his tricks, sang out with a child's bright smile that he had never gone away at all, but that their mother had hidden him deep in the secret part of the cave where he would be safe. And he laughed.

Zan spoke one afternoon to his uncle, Chul, to whom he described these disquieting visions. Chul listened, scratched his bald head, and with open mouth gazed stupidly at the air. Then, slow of speech, he said something he could not know: that Dael was alive. Had he died, Chul said, Zan-Gah would feel it inside. Dael was in some trouble, he thought, and his call for help was reaching Zan-Gah because twins shared a single spirit and were never really apart. This was surely the reason Zan-Gah so often dreamed of him.

Zan left Chul's presence examining his inmost self. He found no message of his brother's death there, and could recall no dream in which Dael had been killed. It was the lioness that was dead. Had Dael died, Zan would surely sense it, but his heart delivered no such report. "If Dael were dead," Zan reasoned, " I would be dead too, for when does a twin long outlive his brother? The great cat had her chance at me but I survived—and so does he! I am certain of it!"

The time had come to tell his mother and father what he intended to do. When he saw them alone he declared in a tone that admitted no contradiction that he would seek his brother, and would not return without him. He told them of his dreams and what his uncle, Chul, had said about them—that they were a cry for help from a twin whose spirit he shared, and that he would answer it or die. Zan did not say that the loss of his brother had been his fault and that, but for a morsel of meat, Dael would be safely home. Nor did he say that he would never feel whole and complete unless he recovered the missing part of himself, but Thal could see that it was so. He knew that each morning Zan awoke with a deep sense of loss because he, Thal, rose with the same bleak and empty feeling. He knew that for Zan it was like the persistent, dull pain of an aching tooth, or the anguish one strangely still feels in a limb that has been lost.

Nevertheless, Thal refused to let Zan go. He answered with an angry outburst, and when Zan stubbornly insisted, Thal actually lifted him up by the shoulders, gazing wildly into his eyes and telling him that he *would not*. But although Zan made no reply, with dismay he saw in the eyes of his son that he *would*. "Father," Zan finally said, and his voice was calm but firm, "Dael calls to me every night in my sleep, and I must answer." Thal did not know what to say. He realized that whatever had happened to Dael could happen to Zan as well, whether

Dael had been killed by a beast, or a man, or was indeed alive and in the hands of enemies. But the boy was unshakable. Zan-Gah was a rock and would not budge nor be dissuaded. This his father also saw.

Wumna, however, knew exactly what she would say. Her "No!" was loud and certain. She too would be a rock! But the rock melted. Falling upon her knees and throwing her arms around her remaining son's waist, she wailed that he would not, could not go, clinging to him as if she meant to hold him on the spot forever. Zan tried to comfort her, feeling real grief that he must so upset his mother, and looking for words that might ease her heartbreak. "Mother, you should be happy—happier than you have been for this whole year. I will be leaving as one and will return as two—I promise." But Zan knew that the words he spoke could well prove untrue, and so did she.

In the end, after much argument, Zan got his parents to the point where, without agreeing or giving in, they said no more in opposition. It was clear that they could not stop the determined lad, and that neither tears nor words would do any good. They began to see a glimmer of hope for Zan's project, and to give credence to Chul's pronouncement that Dael was alive. Maybe he was! The mammoth Chul could be as stupid as he was large, but on those rare occasions when his brute mind engendered an idea, it took on the glow of a prophesy. Chul was consulted and he repeated his words. Zan made ready.

Once the venture was accepted and the family was exchanging views, Thal stated firmly that he would accompany his son. But Zan said, and he saw for himself, that Wumna could not be left behind alone to wonder day and night whether she would ever see any member of her family again. That would be too heavy a burden to place on a woman who was already shattered by the loss of one son. Nor could Chul go, for he had a wife of his own and three girls yet of tender years. They all sat together at their fire and began to make plans for Zan's solitary search.

Zan shared an idea with his family: Often, in the days when he and his brother played and hunted together, Dael had urged him to go further from home than they were allowed. Dael, Zan remembered, had been particularly fascinated by the river, Nobla, that ran nearby. While Zan had always wondered where the current might take him if he would follow its downward flow, Dael (how different the boys were!) always wished that he could follow Nobla to her mysterious *source* in the direction of the distant hills. The thought of finding her birthplace had enthralled Dael. Did the river come from afar in the fading blue beyond or gush from some remote cavern deep in the hollow earth? Some day, Dael had said, they might follow Nobla to her place of birth, hunting and fishing as they went. Perhaps the twins would by this time have begun the adventure if Dael had not vanished from sight.

In trying to decide which way to go in search of him, Zan had to make a difficult decision. Would it not be easier for Dael to have gone with the flow of the river? No, Zan explained to his family, Dael did not care where Nobla went, only where she came from. That is what he always talked about, never the other. He might, in his anger, have decided to make the trip alone instead of sharing it with Zan as he had promised. Zan resolved to travel upstream for eight days, by which time he hoped he would find a clue or sign of Dael. If he did not, he would reverse his direction. Thal and Chul approved. Now Zan-Gah knew where the first step would lead. (He little guessed how far this step would take him, nor what adventures and trials lay ahead!)

Wumna was not slow to point out that every stride might carry him further from his brother, even if he were alive, and that any path was full of dangers. Zan held up his spear, cheerfully reminding his mother that he had slain a lion with it and could as successfully face any other enemy. He was boasting, but he wished to reassure her. Wumna was not comforted. Would he always be as lucky? The clansmen might call him Zan-Gah, but she never once had honored him with that name except with sarcasm. If she spoke it, it was: "Zan-Gah, straighten up the mess you made, Zan-Gah," or she would say: "Zan-Gah, we need more wood, oh mighty warrior." Never was it otherwise. To her he was a boy, not the man he pretended to be, and the search he was now resolved to undertake seemed to her a frightful absurdity that somehow she was powerless to stop.

Zan and his people rose early—Zan to prepare for his journey, and his parents, as well as others of his clan, to help him and to pray for his success. Zan was advised to travel light. He would need his spear and a few other things which he would bring in a pouch made of animal skin. In it he could carry some dried meat, another small skin, some thongs of leather in case he had to tie something, and a stone blade he had laboriously made from a piece of flint. He also had a hollow gourd to carry water, ingeniously fashioned. With regret he left his splendid lion skin in the hands of his uncle, Chul. It was simply too heavy to carry with him. In return Chul gave him a blade shaped of a black, glassy rock that chipped into an extremely sharp instrument. That knife was the finest thing Chul had ever owned. Zan promised to give it back when he returned—if he returned.

As he prepared to bid his son farewell, Zan's father was dejected. He had always labored to protect his family from the terrors of their savage world, but he knew there were some things he could not do. He had been unable to save Dael, and now he was helpless to prevent his other son from doing what he felt he had to do. They had almost lost Zan to the murderous lion—and now?

Wumna began to sob. Would not Zan-Gah delay until the weather was warmer? It was the first time she had seriously given him his title of respect. "Do not mourn for me, Mother," Zan said gently. "Last night as I slept I heard Dael calling to me, and I know his voice will guide me. I will not come home alone."

"You will not come home at all. That is my night dream," she said, weeping so much that hot tears fell upon Zan's shoulder. Chul's wife, Aka, and the oldest of their daughters, who adored Zan, were sniffling too, and others among them joined in the chorus of sobs. Mighty Chul, his own eyes wet, grew angry. Wiping his cheeks with the back of his great fist and thumping the heel of his spear on the ground, he loudly called for silence. Then more softly, but sternly too: "Let there be no weeping. Zan-Gah is going to find his twin brother whom we love. One will depart and two will return. Let us send him on his way."

Thal embraced his son in his strong arms, pressing him against his hairy breast and muttering gruff tendernesses. As Zan gave a final farewell to his family he saw clearly what perhaps he had not seen before—that there was a great strength in living with a people that stood together in difficult times; and that he would now forego that strength, facing a dangerous and hostile world alone. He would not have his father to teach and help him, nor Chul's great strength and protection. His mother who cared about him, loved him, would not be there when he wished for her. For a moment he actually was tempted to put down his spear, stay at home, and be a kid again; but the thoughts and events which had created that moment still urged him on.

Zan embraced his people one by one, Chul last among the men, and finally his mother with a whispered promise to return. It would bring evil luck for any to foresee Zan's project as less than successful, so they held back their questions and fears. As he departed they chanted an ancient song of victory, and lifting their hands to the spirits of the sky, they offered Zan-Gah to their care.

3 THE SLING

Not far from the moist cave that once had been his home there stands to this day a barrow of rocks, worn by time, encrusted with the soil of many centuries, and overgrown with moss and rough vegetation. Under it lie the bones and spear of Zan-Gah. When he died (as everyone someday must), he was widely known and greatly honored, as the huge pile of boulders witnesses. Long after his death, when the elders of his people would recite the deeds of their ancestors—beginning with the great Ack-Ro, who first spoke to the sky-spirits some twenty generations earlier, and Sra-Elod, who learned to make fire—they would not fail to name the deeds of Zan-Gah. Ages after our Zan had passed from the earth, it was still recalled that as a boy he had slain a lioness unaided and had borne her claw marks for the rest of his life. But the greatest of all his accomplishments, the one that changed the lives of his people forever, was something else. It was his invention of the sling. "He fashioned the swift weapon from a serpent's sting," the sages said—and it was partly true. What the old men did not tell when they spoke the long history of their clan, (chanting it, for it was their saga and song), was that Zan came to do it by accident.

It had rained the night before, for the first time in many days—a lucky sign. The drying river was rising again and Zan was cheered by the sweetness of the weather. It was a good time to travel. The birds were deliriously happy about something and the trees were almost in leaf. A gentle southern breeze was at his back and Zan was in very good spirits. Yet he well knew that he must be cautious and stealthy, even though he was still not far from home. The peace between the five clans was an uneasy one, for many still carried old grudges born of blood-strife. Zan wished he could proceed without being observed, but it made sense to follow the river, where game was likely to come and fish could be speared. Nobla would always give him water, and that was even more important than meat. But for the same reasons people—enemies—might come there too.

The river would take him north and then turn to the west in a wide arc. That much he knew. Just as it was beginning to curve Zan would encounter the dwellings of the two northern clans, and he was resolved to visit them. Zan wished to speak to the white-haired Aniah, to inquire of Dael and seek the elder's advice. Aniah, who had been the first to address him as Zan-Gah, would receive him, Zan thought, in spite of the antique quarrels that rooted in the minds of old men.

But before that he would try to see the people of Hru. Zan was more hopeful about Aniah than he was of the Hru, but if he followed the river he would encounter them first. Of all the clans, the Hru were the least friendly and the soonest to quarrel over an imaginary insult or some trifle. Zan wondered whether he should bypass them entirely. It was not likely that they would know anything about Dael, nor that they would tell him if they did. The Hru kept to themselves. Deeds of courtesy were unknown to them, and generosity was rarely to be seen in their brute lives. Zan did want to pursue every possible lead, so he decided to attempt a visit, but he knew there was the danger of rebuff—or worse. He gripped his spear with resolution, and at the same time hoped he would not have to use it.

Meanwhile, Zan resolved to enjoy his freedom. His father would not be telling him what to do, and his mother was not there to weep and tremble over his every step. Their parting had been sad, but being gone, he was inclined to look on the happier side of things. This would be an adventure! He felt the fresh air in his nostrils and enjoyed the bright sunshine of the clear blue sky. When he glanced at Nobla's sparkling stream, he could almost see his cheerful brother spearing fish in it. Zan allowed himself to hope that he would find Dael before long.

After several hours of walking, he decided to rest and eat some of the food he had brought. He was about to sit on a flat shelf of rock a few steps ahead when he heard a sound that chilled his blood and caused his hair to stand on end. It was the muffled hiss of a snake. Zan froze in his steps and searched for it, trying to move nothing but his eyes. He did not see immediately where the noise had come from, and dared not move until he did. The hissing noise began again, and Zan could now see that the serpent was a poisonous one. It was coiled directly in front of him! Zan stared at the snake and the snake stared at him, and neither seemed to know what to do.

Zan's heart leapt to his throat and pounded there. His mouth went dry. The serpent might strike at any moment! Once his uncle Chul had been bitten by a snake and had lain sick for many days. He had been saved from death by his powerful constitution and the care of his family. Zan, far from home, knew that he probably would die if he were bitten, but what could he do to prevent it? He could only back away a little at a time, hoping that the reptile would not be provoked into striking. Then as he began to withdraw, stepping very slowly backwards, he noticed that the snake had a bird, half swallowed and still fluttering in its jaws.

Those creatures have mouths that can open so wide that they can swallow small animals whole. With great relief Zan realized that this snake would be unable to bite him because it was gorging on something else. This changed everything. It was the snake that was in danger now! Although it might try and even succeed in scratching him with a poisonous fang, it was open to attack. Backing off slowly, Zan made a wide half-circle around it. Then with a movement that had to be swift, Zan, in a single motion, seized the snake's tail with a firm grip and whipped its head against the stone. Its neck was instantly broken, but Zan repeated the action three or four times until it was as limp as a piece of rope. Then for a few moments he left the body lie, observing it for any movement and cautiously poking it with his spear to make sure that it was dead. The bird could not be saved.

Dinner! Snake meat can be perfectly good to eat, even if its bite is poisonous. With the sharp stone blade Chul had given him, Zan cut off the head and hurled it away with the bird still in its mouth. He slit open the belly so that he could peel away the skin in a single piece, looking at it with some admiration. In spite of its venomous bite, this was a handsome animal with rich geometric patterns decorating its slender body. He would save and use the skin, but first he must eat.

With effort he built a fire and roasted the meat on his spear. He ate some, and some he kept in his sack for later. For a while after his meal Zan lay on his back under a tree which gave him shelter from the glaring afternoon sun and watched the light peeking through the leaves as they moved. He was happy. He thought he had never tasted anything so delicious, but more important, he had passed two significant tests. He had defended himself from danger and had provided himself with food. Not bad! Too bad Chul had not been there to see him!

But the day was advancing and he still hoped to reach the Hru clan before night. Zan had work to do. He turned his attention to the snake skin, which had to be cleaned and prepared for use. He scraped the inside of the skin with his blade and rubbed it back and forth around the trunk of a slender tree with both hands to turn it into a flexible leather-like strip. He did not know what he would do with it but it was beautiful and a thing to prize.

Perhaps he would make a gift of it to Aniah, whose help he sought, or maybe he would trade it for something he needed. For the time being he could wear it as a sash, and so he did as he lifted his spear and went on.

In every new invention there is apt to be a certain serendipity—that is, a sudden, unlikely stroke of luck that makes all the difference. This is what happened: At a point where Zan was fairly close to the river, he came upon an area moistened by the recent rains where grew a bed of low-lying broadleaf plants. He recognized the plants. They had large, white flowers below their dark leaves which early developed into a tasty fruit—the first of the season. There they were, thousands of them. Zan started gathering the largest ones, which were about the size of walnuts, stuffing them into his bag. But the bag had already been full, so there was not much room. He did not want to empty it to hold more fruit, but he did not wish to abandon the surplus either; so he looked for another way to carry some. He would be needing his goatskin for warmth that night, but he lit upon the idea of wrapping some of the fruit in the snakeskin. Unfortunately, the skin was long and narrow, although fairly wide at one end. No, it wouldn't do. But it was all Zan had, so he loosely enclosed several of the nuggets and went on with the imperfect bundle in his free hand.

He had not progressed many steps when he realized that the objects were falling out of the clumsy container. He gathered up those that had fallen, rewrapped them, and progressed as best he could, stopping frequently to pick up those that refused to stay in their package. Zan ate a couple because he saw that he would lose them anyway, and after a half hour he looked at the bundle and discovered that he had indeed lost them. All but one had dropped along the way! Zan was furious! He took the snakeskin with its one remaining fruit, twirled it over his head, and threw it away with all his might.

Then something unexpected happened. Serendipity! The small end of the snakeskin, still wound around Zan's finger, stayed with him, but the round fruit flew like a shot against a large boulder and was smashed, so that it left its juice running down the side.

Zan marveled at what he had done. Was it just his anger? He decided to attempt more calmly to duplicate what he had done in rage. Picking up a sharp stone, he placed it in the center of the strip of skin, wrapping the smaller end around his forefinger. Then he whirled it vigorously over his head and let it go. The stone flew with such force that the sharp edge stuck deeply in the bark of an oak tree. Zan examined the embedded stone with astonishment. What if this tree trunk were a man—an enemy? This could be a weapon as dangerous as a spear! But could it be controlled like a spear? Zan tried again without much success. It was awkward to handle. He tried several times with varying results. Even when the stone was released properly it was difficult to aim, and the snakeskin was beginning to fray. It would tear apart soon.

Zan realized that he would have to fashion this weapon, this sling, of stronger materials. He did not wish to cut up his goatskin, but a leg of it could be spared, so he cut off a patch only about the size of his hand. To it he tied a long thong or strap (which he luckily had brought with him) on either side of the patch. It would work better than the snakeskin. The piece would hold the stone and the thongs would allow him to whirl it overhead even faster than before. And it would last much longer.

By the time Zan finished making his sling it was almost dark. The Hru would have to wait. He tried his weapon and it worked! He could not see any more where the stone went, but he heard it zing and crash in the brush. Zan was eager to practice in order to become proficient at its use, but it was too dark to see what he was doing. He had to arrange some shelter for himself, build another fire, and get some sleep. He set up next to the large stone where he had so luckily smashed the piece of fruit. It was still stuck there, and Zan pulled it away and ate it.

Zan could hardly sleep, so thrilled was he with his discovery. Of course he realized that it needed to be worked on, to be perfected. He longed for the coming of the morning. Lying on his back and staring upward at the gorgeous multitude of stars, he thought with excitement of the possibilities of his invention. Then he thought of his family and of Dael. Suddenly a shooting star streaked across the sky, like a blazing stone flung against the black void of the universe. It was truly a happy sign, for Zan knew by this heavenly assurance that his new project would succeed. It was his destiny.

4 THE HRU

Zan fairly leapt up with the first light of day. He immediately thought of the wonderful shooting star hurtling across the sky—at the very time he had been working on his own hurler of rocks. The omen, as brief as it was beautiful, gleamed in his memory. But would the sling work as it had seemed to the day before? Zan was almost afraid to try it for fear of disappointment. So he ate his fruit and cold snake flesh, and drank deeply from the river Nobla. At its bank he carefully selected some smooth stones, foreseeing that sharp or uneven ones would be harder to throw accurately, and might cut the weapon before he had learned to use it. He knew that practice—maybe a day's or maybe a week's—would be necessary to master its use. When his father had shown him how to fish with his bare hands, Zan had only caused the experienced Thal to laugh when he tried it; but in a week's time, with constant effort, he was as good as Thal, or even better. It had been the same earlier, when he and Dael began to fish with their father's spears. Practice, only practice, made them good at it. It would be the same with the sling.

Zan tried his invention several times, winding it over his head energetically and releasing the stone with its characteristic *whizz* and *thud*. What a powerful thing it was! But it was clumsy and hard to control. He discovered that it worked better when the thongs were a little shorter, and he learned to avoid entangling his arm or hitting his head with the strap; but it took long hours of trial to perfect its use. First he tried whirling the sling overhead, then side-arm. He had his best success when he began with the stone draped over his shoulder and behind, taking a run and flinging it forcefully above his head while bending his knees and putting his whole body into the motion. Sometimes he whirled it more than once to assess the target and get the feel of the stone he was using, but found that it was a single, strong throw from behind his back and overhead that sent it flying. A wind-up was not really necessary. Much practice and experimentation perfected the release. He had to hold on to one strap while letting the other go at exactly the right moment, so he tied a loop for his third finger (the third worked best) in the longer strap. Now he could release only one strap, while the other stayed attached to his hand. He tried different kinds of rocks too, determining which size was best. Smooth round stones proved the most reliable. But timing was everything. Only as the evening approached, after long hours of experimentation, practice, and repetition, did Zan begin to hit the targets he had set up for himself with any regularity.

Then Zan rested. His arm would be sore the next day. He sheltered himself under the shadow of his rock, searched his packet for the little remaining food, and quietly ate. The sun was going down and not a sound could be heard except for insects and the muffled noise of Zan's chewing. Three rabbits appeared from nowhere, as they are apt to do toward dusk. They ignored Zan's silent presence, but he did not ignore theirs! Soundlessly reaching for his sling with one hand and a stone with the other, and concentrating on the closest animal, Zan very slowly got up. Sensing danger, all three rabbits froze. The sun shone through their long ears and made them glow bright red. Readying the sling behind him, Zan flung it with a whir at one of the rabbits perhaps fifteen paces away—and missed. The three rabbits were slightly startled at the sound, but Zan stopped moving and stood still as the trunk of a tree. All was quiet again. The animal Zan had aimed at was curiously unaware of what was happening and how narrowly it had escaped (for the aim was not far off). It hopped a few feet and continued eating the green, new grass. Zan would get another shot, and this time he did not miss! He would have more meat to eat, and a soft rabbit skin to use or trade.

As he took up the slain animal Zan was greatly pleased with himself. He felt increased confidence to be in possession of this new, swift weapon which he was learning to use so skillfully. It had the advantage of being easily and secretly carried. He could wear it like a belt or wind it up into a small package and none would know that he had it. Meanwhile, he held his spear to discourage attack—for attacked he would be if enemies thought him unarmed. Zan did not have to wait long for a chance to use his weapons.

It would still be light for an hour or two and Zan, who had not planned such a long delay, decided to approach the dwelling place of the Hru while he still could. Perhaps they would give him a night's lodging before they sent him on his way. In these circumstances it was best to offer the rabbit as a gift, rather than keeping it for himself, so holding it by its hind legs and tossing it over his shoulder, he gathered his things and marched on.

Zan was not sure how far he had to go, and as he walked he considered how to approach this unfriendly and troublesome group. He suddenly felt the sharp sting of a rock in the middle of his back, and guessed that he had arrived. He turned to see who had flung it at him and saw two scraggly boys—one of about his age and another that looked like the younger brother—both glowering at him as if Zan were their worst enemy. The elder of the two let out an unnatural, shrill scream that was intended to frighten, but Zan could see that the boy himself was scared.

Zan knew how to deal with this kind of assault. He had his sling and could repel the puny threat with stunning force. Indeed, as Zan reflected, he could probably kill them both. But did he want to? The sling was powerful enough, and he had his sharp-pointed spear too. However, Zan had not come there to fight children, nor to open old wounds that might well renew a war that had quietly gone to sleep. Besides, he feared that if he used the new weapon, his enemies might soon figure it out and make it for themselves. Then everybody would be endangered.

So Zan resisted the strong temptation to retaliate and let pass an opportunity to use his new-found power. Still, he had to do something, so with a loud yell he charged the two with his spear as if he meant indeed to kill them with it. The boys did exactly what Zan had learned not to do—they turned and ran for a hiding place in the woods. It was fortunate for them that Zan intended them no harm, because in running they completely exposed themselves to Zan's spear. However, Zan only wished to chase them away.

It was not long after that he came upon the Hru families sheltered in a hollow place beneath a stone cliff. The area was three-quarters enclosed by a bend in the river, with the cliff a short distance away. Long ago the river had run in the very place where they now made their camp, but having changed its course, it left behind this hollow place—a fit enough shelter, unless too-heavy rains came to wash them away from their own beds. As soon as Zan approached he saw that things had gone badly for them. They were so gaunt that their ribs and other bones stood out on their bodies, and their eyes seemed hollow and dull. The babies were crying, and Zan was appalled to see that their small stomachs were swollen. A disgusting smell greeted his nostrils.

Both the women and the men were listless and weak. Flies settled on their faces and eyes and they did not even brush them off, either because they were too feeble or just did not care. Without rising, the men made weakly gestures for Zan to go away, and offered him the same piercing and unearthly howl that he had heard shortly before. One of the clansmen took up his spear although he seemed little inclined to use it. Others just stared at him with hostile, bloodshot eyes bulging from empty sockets. Zan started to speak but they continued to shoo him and to scream with hoarse voices the same unholy sound. One man (possibly their leader) rose with some effort, turned his back to Zan, and brushed his feet on the ground, kicking dust in Zan's direction.

It was obvious that Zan would get no help from them. At their best they were suspicious of strangers. Now, too weak to whisk away flies, they used the little strength they had to send him despitefully on his way. Just as he turned to leave, the two boys who had thrown rocks at him arrived. Not yet as frail as the others, they apparently had been foraging for food when Zan had come upon them. They were startled to see him again and stepped a little backwards in fright. In pure pity Zan walked up to them, handed them the rabbit he had brought down with his sling, and left. Turning around after a moment or two to look back at these miserable wretches, he saw that they had already fallen on the rabbit and were tearing at it like animals with their bare hands and teeth. They were starving.

Why were the Hru unable to feed themselves when Zan alone had succeeded in getting food in abundance as soon as he had begun his journey? It happened sometimes. The men of Hru had been unlucky in the hunt, and once they were weak with hunger their chances of success rapidly diminished to nothing. As far as Zan could see, they were simply waiting to die. Zan reflected that the gift he had given might well have saved the entire clan. He hoped so, for he did not feel hate but only sorrow for them. Still, he thought to himself, they probably would continue to hate and fear him as much as ever.

It was almost night and Zan needed a place to sleep. Thal had often advised him to select a place of safety rather than comfort. Safety *was* comfort, as his father had often said. It was best, he knew, not to be too much in the open because hunters might find him sleeping and at their mercy. When Zan saw a large pine tree, its branches hanging to the ground, he recognized the kind of place Thal had taught him to seek. There, beneath the tree, he would be completely out of sight, and the fallen needles would make a soft bed too. So Zan camped there, but he dared not light a fire lest he be seen from a distance. He had no desire to be a meal for the desperate Hru should they recover enough of their strength to find him and fall upon him. Best to disappear for the night.

When he awoke the next morning he was well rested, and peering through the branches for safety, he emerged from his hideaway and began hiking in the direction of the northern clan. At about noon, near a stand of lofty poplars, he came upon a dozen handsome young men, tall and well-built. As soon as they saw him they stood together, seizing their weapons and facing him. Zan continued to advance toward them, feeling fairly sure that they were the people he was looking for. He hoped he would not have to fight them but who knew? The clans seemed always to be on edge, belligerent to strangers and ever ready for a brawl. At once, spears and clubs in hand, they formed a ring around Zan, frowning deeply. As he turned to look at them, the circle of men rotated around him. They could easily have finished him at any time, but Zan didn't think they would. "He is too small to eat," one of them said, and they all laughed. Another thrust toward Zan with his spear to see if he could make him flinch, but Zan looked straight into his eyes and moved not a bit. Still another tried the same trick, and Zan faced him down without the slightest movement. Impressed though they were, the young fellows were still inclined to have a little fun at Zan's expense; but then someone noticed his scars—dark ribbons on his arms and across his shoulders. "It is Zan-Gah!" he heard someone say. "See his wounds!" "It is Zan-Gah who killed the lion!" A buzz of whispers followed, and Zan saw their hostility turn to friendly curiosity. Lowering their weapons, they examined his scars and his spear, and seemed not to know what to say until the oldest (so he appeared) said "Welcome, Zan-Gah!"—and all of the young men greeted him warmly, some even putting their arms around him and leading him like a hero and a brother to their camp.

The older tribesmen turned out to see what the commotion was, while several young girls peeked out at him with wonder. "This is Zan-Gah who killed the lion," he heard again, highly pleased in spite of himself. Then, facing a leader of the tribe he said, "I seek Aniah, if he will speak with me."

5 ANIAH

"Aniah has gone to hunt," a dark-bearded man said. "Stay and eat with us and perhaps he will return." They did not have much to offer, but were pleased to share what they had with Zan-Gah. While they were nibbling a few nuts and seeds saved from the previous year, an elderly man arrived carrying a deer as big as himself on his shoulders. It was Aniah. How he had managed alone to kill the nimble animal using only his spear was a mystery to Zan. One young man, guessing his thought, leaned toward Zan and whispered in his ear: "We do not know how he does it either. He always goes out alone. He is the greatest hunter who ever lived. And he is old! Look at him!"

Zan looked and saw a sinewy, fleshless man, stooped and white-haired—about seventy-five. Age had twisted his hands into knots, and his skin hung loosely on his wrinkled face and body; but there was a vigor in his step and expression that suggested a great enjoyment of life however old he might be. Aniah flung the deer down at the feet of the seated men, chuckling softly. "You ancient fellows may sit here relaxing," he seemed to say, "but we *young men* have to find something to eat."—and with a twinkle he tossed his great-grandchild a piece of fruit hidden in his hand. (It was the same kind that had luckily enabled Zan to invent his sling.)

"Well, young fellow," said he, his eyes falling on the visitor. "What brings Zan-Gah away from his comfortable home? No, do not tell me now. We will eat first, and then you may declare your errand."

While the deer was being prepared for roasting, Aniah donned a majestic dappled fur, and seating himself in his accustomed place, he looked like what he was—a king among his people. Zan knew that he must approach Aniah with great respect but no hint of fear. That, indeed, was the way everybody treated him—except for his great-grandson who, without ceremony, plopped himself into Aniah's lap and began tugging on his white beard.

Meanwhile, Zan was drawn away by the younger men to participate in a friendly tug-of-war. They usually had their contest stretching a length of strong vine over a pit of hot coals—no gentle sport—but the fire was being used to roast a haunch of venison, so they put the two competing teams on either side of an inlet where water from the river jutted inland. The losing group, or at least its leader, would either let go of the vine or go tumbling into the water. Zan was placed in the midst of one team—among the smallest lads of either group. What sport, what heroic effort, and what laughter as now one team lost, now another! Zan was a kid again, laughing and screaming; and all the while Aniah looked on and laughed too. The rich odor of roasted meat soon drew the youths from their game, and the girls, who had been busy in preparations, seized the long vine and engaged in the same contest with loud cheers and shrieking laughter.

When the food was ready, all were seated and Aniah gave out portions, serving Zan first and himself last. None put food to his mouth until Aniah began to eat, and then a symphony of munching followed. When all had eaten their fill, Aniah turned toward Zan and waited. Laying his spear at the elder's feet and placing his knuckles on his chest, Zan bowed his head in obeisance. "Great Aniah, I thank you for the welcome you have given me." Zan raised his eyes and watched Aniah carefully. "You know my brother, who twinned with me, is lost. I believe he still lives, and I seek him."

"Why here?" Aniah replied sharply. Zan saw him stiffen. "We do not hold him." He held up his withered hands as if to show that they were empty.

"Great leader, that mistrust never came to my mind. I visit you because you are famed to know the many secrets of earth and sky. I did not wish to undertake a search without asking for your help and advice. And because I received from you my name of honor, I decided to turn to you as to a friend."

Aniah looked at the young man in front of him and smiled a strange, questioning smile, as of one who looks into the abyss of time and sees himself many long years earlier. "When your brother was lost, we all tried to find him, the same as if he had been one of our own. No one knows what happened. I wish the birds would speak to me, as you seem to think they do, and then I would know. But yes, we have our suspicions."

In answer to Zan's attentive and inquiring look, Aniah went on: "For several years now, and not for the first time, we have had encounters with the wasp men. They live many days off, deep in the blue hills, and yet they come marauding here. They hunt in our lands, they take what does not belong to them, and on one occasion (I know for a certainty), they carried away a woman of the Luta clan. I heard long ago that they were robbers and slavers too. These are fierce and dangerous warriors, but as long as they stayed far from us we were not much concerned about them."

Zan's eyes lit up. "Do you think that...."

"Yes, Dael was alone when he was lost, was he not?"

"We think he may have been traveling up Nobla. He often said he would find her source."

"If so, he was heading straight for the dwellings of the wasp people! What you say confirms my thought, Zan-Gah. I have long suspected that he was their captive. That is the best explanation of his disappearance—but it is only a guess. I know no more than you."

"Why do you call them 'wasp people'?" Zan asked.

"They claim an ancient relationship with actual wasps and say they are of their tribe. These people do not live in cave shelters as we do, but build great, bulbous hollows out of trees, bark, and leaves. They look exactly like enormous nests of wasps, as they are intended to. The entrance is but a small round hole on the end of it. If someone unwelcome approaches, they lie there silent and motionless until the intruder is near. Then they swarm out, one after another, screaming, spears in their hands to attack and overwhelm the unlucky visitor. They tip their spears with poison, like a wasp's sting, so that the smallest wound becomes terribly painful and disabling— although the poison itself does not kill. I think the wasp men would rather wound than kill, so that they can take prisoners as slaves."

"The people you describe are truly like stinging hornets," Zan said thoughtfully. "My hair stands on end to hear you speak of them. My uncle, Chul...."

"Chul." Aniah's eyes darkened for the briefest moment. Zan went on cautiously, sensing that he was touching a tender place: "He told me that there had once been an invasion by a distant people, and that the clans united against them."

"Yes," Aniah recalled, his brow smoothing again. "That was one of the few times that our five clans stood together. We could never have repelled them otherwise. They were many and dangerous."

Zan told Aniah about his experience with the Hru, how ill they had received him, and of their miserable condition. The old man's face assumed an expression of contempt. "The Hru are a low people, thieves and cowards all. I do not pity them."

In the course of their conversation, which became relaxed and friendly, Zan expressed admiration for Aniah's skill as a hunter. How, he could not resist asking, had he managed to kill a deer without any assistance?

"One should pursue good fortune with vigor and action," he answered, "but sometimes the secret is to wait until good fortune comes to you." He laughed his soft, chuckling laugh. As they conversed, Zan was surprised to discover that this great leader was in some respects a simple man, cheerful and good-humored. He liked a joke and could tell a story. And he had a way of laughing as if at something that had happened long ago.

Zan grew bolder: "Tell me, Aniah, why have the clans so often been enemies? What mischief could have caused our peoples to make war against one another? It is as if we were haunted by a strange secret that no one speaks of but everyone knows."

"Not everyone, Zan-Gah." Aniah replied ruefully. "My father knew, but most of those who first fought in the quarrel have died—some of old age! I think the war eventually stopped because most of us forgot why we were fighting. And there was the drought. Our struggle then was only to survive; and in our search for water and food we were forced to move away, beyond each other's reach. When the rains finally came, and we returned, none had the stomach for war and killing any longer. That is not so long ago. That is within your young lifetime."

"But what could have started it," Zan inquired earnestly, "or have kept it alive so many years?"

"I was hardly older then than you are now when it began." Aniah's face became tight and grim, and he looked straight ahead. Red bonfires gleamed in his eyes. "One of the southern tribesmen stole a woman of Hru. Foh! Why would he want her? But her husband wanted her back and she refused to go back. Perhaps she was pretty, but her man was a cruel brute. An animal treats his mate better! I have always avoided hatred, even of the enemies of my people, but I cannot purge myself of my detestation of the Hru! The war could have been avoided entirely but for her blunt-brained husband who could not be pacified—no, not by the promise of many gifts. He wanted back what everyone knew he did not love or value.

"In those days the Hru were not the pitiable lot that you saw when you were in their camp yesterday. Back then they were the strongest and most numerous of the clans. The husband (his name was Bruah) rallied several of his assassin tribe and they looked for an opportunity to avenge themselves for the insult (as they considered it). Down they went to the southern forest and prepared an ambush—not for the offender, but for anyone who passed! The first to die was your grandfather's father. They fell on that good man and killed him with their spears; and boasted of it too, so that word spread of what had happened. It was not very long before the clans chose sides. You of the three southern clans stood together."

"And you of the north?"

"It was not my choice. I was but a lad. Our elders made the decision, and it surely was a difficult one. It seemed imprudent at the time to oppose our powerful neighbors in order to uphold the stealing of a woman, although we knew the circumstances. We found ourselves supporting the Hru. In time we were sorry because once bands of men began marauding, they attacked anyone who was in their path. You could not go hunting without wondering whether you were being hunted. Pretty soon our women were being carried off, and not by our enemies! If one of ours can be stolen, the men of Hru reasoned, why not one of theirs? So they attacked their own allies! Fools and scoundrels both!"

Aniah continued: "Soon all of the clans were at odds with one another, and we knew not in which direction to point our spears. Strangely enough, that had the effect of slowing the conflict, and there were long periods of a hostile sort of peace—intermissions that were suddenly broken by some wanton act or other crying out for revenge. There were fights over hunting territories and the best dwelling places. But after a time the chief motive was simply a desire to avenge deeds that themselves had been acts of vengeance."

"Did anyone avenge my great-grandfather's murder?" Zan asked.

"Blood takes a long time to dry, Zan-Gah. I cannot describe to you the rage for vengeance that that act begot! But the northern tribes were wary of reprisal. For a long time nothing happened, and things quieted down. Meanwhile, we had to venture out if only for food. It was several years later when it began again. I was hunting with a favorite kinsman in pursuit of a boar—delicious eating, if the boar doesn't eat you! We had gotten careless. My friend had run ahead, and suddenly there appeared in front of him an enormous, a *gigantic* man. My comrade was of slight build and had no chance against the giant, who struck him dead with his club. I confronted the slayer but he was able to knock away my spear and we wrestled for our lives. I barely managed to escape from the powerful grip of...."

"Of...."

"Of your uncle, Chul."

Zan's heart sank. "Aniah, you know I love my uncle and regard him as a great man. Truly, I would fight with him and die for him, whatever the cause."

"I do not hate him," Aniah replied. "Time and advanced age have made me less eager for a fight than I once was. How many good men were lost in needless battles! My kinsman, as I told you, was killed at the height of his manhood. I am old now and have learned to love peace and the company of my grandchildren. But somewhere among the five clans is a warrior who still dreams of revenge, and one act of vengeance gives birth to many others."

"Perhaps my twin brother was killed for revenge," Zan suggested mournfully.

"No, Zan-Gah. To make vengeance good, his body would have been left where your family could find it. Besides, throughout this long war children were never attacked. Never once! Even the detestable Hru would not do that. Still, you should be careful. The wasp people do not spare the young, and I think they have made a slave of your brother. I would advise you to save yourself and return to your home, but I know you must and you will seek him. That is why I respect you, young as you are. But fear the spirits most when they are excessively kind. So far you have been fortunate." Zan thought of the lucky invention of his new weapon. "And beware the wasp people. They are a fierce enemy, treacherous, shrewd, and full of guile. If they find you spying on them, you will not escape the touch of their stinging spears, nor the sure captivity that follows. Hate them, if anybody in the world, Zan-Gah, and fear them!"

"My fear is for my brother, Dael, who never encountered unkindness and was incapable of it himself. What should so gentle a person do among the tortures of the wasp men? I think that all I will find will be his memory."

"A young man receives a call from the spirits to seek and help his brother, and no brother is closer than a twin. You have a long trek before you, Zan-Gah, a journey of many days. First you will have to cross a deep gorge and pass through the land of red rocks. The wasp men hive in the blue hills beyond. If you go farther than these hills you come to a great waste, a deadly desert. Do not go where none can live."

"Aniah," Zan said with some hesitation, "let us at least be friends. We drink from the same river and warm ourselves with the same sun. We face the same perils and rejoice with the very same songs. Is that not a beginning? When I return with my brother, we will show our friendship by visiting you."

Aniah rose and led Zan to a new fire enjoyed by the younger men. Several of them offered presents to Zan, mostly stone blades, but he told them to save their gifts for the time of his return because he dared not take on any additional weight. The gift of Aniah he did not refuse. It was a kit for making fire, consisting of a straight, pointed stick, a strap, and two small blocks of wood, plus some very dry grass. Robo, Aniah's youngest son (the man with a dark beard) showed Zan how to use it. What a treasure! Zan had seen nothing like it before. It would enable him to make fire in moments, whenever he needed it. As he had planned, Zan gave Aniah the snake skin, which the old man took with pleasure, for it was very handsome.

Sitting around the fire, which threw a shower of sparks into the night air when someone added fuel, one lad began to tap a rhythm on a hollow log. Then a second coaxed out a duller sound, each drummer alternating the sounds he made with the percussion of the other, *tip TAH, tip TAH, tip TAH tip TAH tip TAH.* Their drums soon split the air, and these men of the north loved to sing! Their chant is now many thousands of years old:

Live bravely friend!

Live well to the end!

For no man lives forever!

The next morning Zan-Gah bade farewell to the people of the northern clan.

6 THE LAND OF RED ROCKS

As Zan began his trek over a vast grassland, he could see that his new battle would be with the land, and that it might prove a bitter fight. The weather had changed. A persistent wind blew at his back as he walked, whipping the tall grass and chilling his body. The river was to his right with its border of trees, but on his left little grew but grass, except for an occasional dying tree raising its black branches against the sky. Zan strode along with vigorous and consistent steps across the empty land. In time he found a footpath which he was glad to use, even though it increased his exposure to danger. The feet of strangers had worn this path, not those of friends. As he walked Zan began to wonder whether he was hearing his own footsteps or those of another. He could not feel easy until the path, which was old and little employed, disappeared and left him on an empty field again.

Up to this point Nobla had been Zan's guide, but when he came to a fork in the river he had to choose which branch to follow. Considering in his mind what Dael would have done, he decided to stay with the branch on his own side. He followed it for a whole day, leaving the other stream far away. Yet he worried that he should perhaps have taken the other; the one he was on twisted and turned constantly, lengthening his journey. After a while it reduced to a slight flow and began to turn sharply toward the direction from which he had come. It was useless to follow it any more. Zan crossed the waning stream and resumed his approximate path across the featureless plain.

For two nights Zan built his fires from the sparsest materials and slept in ruts padded with grass. He wished he could be more comfortable, but he did not expect it here. His aim now was not to achieve comfort but to keep himself alive. That required water, food, and shelter—and a sharp eye against enemies. He began to regret that he had left the river, but when he awoke on the third morning a heavy dew had left the various grasses dripping with moisture and Zan was able to refresh himself. There was no food, however.

Zan knew that he had to find something to eat, but his need was not urgent. With any luck there would be seeds or berries along the way, and eventually he would kill a rabbit, which was stupid, or a possum, which was slow. It seemed to him as he progressed that the earth he tread on was almost alive, whispering to him, a stubborn and willful creature to be dealt with each day anew. For a long time the ground was perfectly flat; then suddenly the platform of the earth dropped off for several feet as if the entire prairie had caved in ages before and was trying ever since to recover itself. As further evidence of its freakish nature, there lay in a gorge ahead (dug by who knew what invisible force) an enormous skeleton embedded in the ground. Zan climbed down to examine the mastodon, whose ribs and curling tusks, whitened by an age of suns, rose over his head and stood out against the empty sky.

Crouching slightly, Zan could fit within the hollow cage of its upward-pointing ribs, and was amused to enter when to his surprise a live animal waddled out of it! It was a porcupine with bristling needles, and Zan stepped out of its way, at the same time readying his spear and quickly finishing it off. He would have meat again, but to cook it required wood. Fortunately he saw a dead tree at the top of a rise, so he walked there to get some, then to eat, and to rest. From this higher level he could see for a considerable distance, mostly high grass, but in the very direction he had been heading he saw—what he had not seen for days—a winding row of trees. It looked as if he had found Nobla again—the fork he had not taken.

It was almost night when he approached the trees, but enough light remained to observe a strange circumstance. Every branch of every tree was covered, even to the lofty tops, with a broad-leafed vine. Late as it was, it was a ghostly sight. They were enveloped and almost swallowed by this invader, so that they looked more like dark green hills or mounds than trees with branches and leaves of their own. Zan was a little frightened at this unfamiliar sight, but Nobla was in all probability on the other side of it, so he pushed the vines aside and entered the cradled emptiness. It took a moment for his eyes to adjust to the dimness. With amazement he made out a spacious dome above supported by the now visible branches—for looking up it was still a little light, whereas darkness surrounded him like smoke in the lower reaches of this sanctuary.

Zan decided to go no further. He leaned against the slightly sloping trunk of a sycamore and began to doze. He was profoundly tired and he would be safe here, hidden from stranger eyes. But was he mistaken or did he hear something rustling in the bed of fallen leaves? And now a whimpering sound! What was it? Startled and affrighted, Zan reached for his spear—and felt something warm. It was a human foot! Zan almost fainted when, as he grabbed the ankle, he heard a wild scream of fear. It was a child, judging by the voice and the smallness of the limb. Whatever or whoever it was, it continued to scream in sheer terror, as if a wild animal had seized it in its jaws and would certainly devour it alive.

It was absolutely dark now, and Zan, unable to see, and afraid to let the small being go for fear that it would bring others, grabbed the child in his arms and tried to comfort it. He gently hushed it, stroking the forehead soothingly and assuring the child that all would be well. The terrified child was trying to bite Zan, and it was a long time before Zan could calm the youngster and convince this intruder that there was no danger. Eventually the child slept, exhausted by the powerful emotions it had experienced, and Zan slept too.

Zan was awakened the next morning by the sound of the waif searching his sack for food. He looked at him for a moment, seeing that it was a boy about two years younger than himself. When the child became aware

of Zan's glance he was alarmed and darted off, but Zan
caught him and again calmed him down, offering a piece
of roasted meat left from the day before. The child, ugly,
ragged and dirty, was hungry to the point of starvation.
Zan tried to talk to him as he ate but the boy spoke a
different language. Yet his speech was not so different
from Zan's that he was impossible to understand at all.
Indeed, Zan had at first thought the boy simply had
difficulty speaking clearly. In time Zan was able to convey
his own name and learn the other's, which sounded like
"Rydl". At first the lad had been reluctant to tell his name,
as if it might give Zan power over him, but in time he
came to trust Zan a little. It took a good deal of effort
for either to make out anything the other said. Zan tried
to tell him that he was in search of his twin brother, and
to inquire whether he had seen him, but Rydl seemed
unable to comprehend "twin," and that was that.

This Zan did learn: that Rydl was of the wasp people,
and lost for many days. At first he was a runaway, but
when he had decided to return he had lost his sense of
direction and traveled farther and farther from home. The
poor fellow had stayed alive by eating insects—beetles,
ants, and grasshoppers. Zan immediately determined to
take the youngster with him. When he came to the land of
the wasp men they might be more willing to receive and
help him if he brought back a missing child. That would
be better than a gift. Zan asked Rydl to point where he
thought he had come from. With some uncertainty, Rydl
pointed toward Zan's dwelling. No wonder he was lost!

As the traveler prepared to depart, his new companion
lost his fear of him and trailed after his footsteps like

a puppy. Zan would have no trouble bringing the boy along. Zan had only a rough idea of his way, but that was more than Rydl could contribute, so Rydl followed Zan, a few paces behind. The young fellow did nothing but chatter, as if his long isolation and pent-up anxieties were terribly in need of release now that he felt out of danger. Zan could understand little of what he said, and even when the boy lagged well behind, and could not be heard anyway, still he talked and talked. Zan understood his need if not his speech, and was actually very glad to have company. He decided to attempt conversation, so he slowed down and allowed the lad to catch up with him. In a couple of days of travel across the grassland together, Zan could catch most of what was said because their languages were related—similar if not the same. Rydl was even quicker to pick up Zan's words, and as each tried to use the other's speech, they arrived at a workable mixture of their two languages.

Nobla was again left far behind. The grassland gradually gave way to a different kind of growth, a rough shrub which dotted the land with dark green patches against a dusty soil. Then the soil itself changed to a different, redder hue. For two more days Zan and his companion trod this jagged and dusty terrain. There were no more trees, only the scruffy bushes and rocks. On the afternoon of the second day, when the weary repetition of footsteps hypnotized Zan into carelessness, he was violently brought back to himself by the sudden presence of an incredibly deep gorge, a split in the earth so profound that he could scarcely see the bottom of it. Its abrupt appearance was completely unexpected, and he almost stepped in. That would have been the end of Zan-Gah! Zan lay down and peered over the edge. The gulch seemed bottomless. Cliff-dwelling birds could be seen flying within and crying around their nests, while a pair of enormous vultures with ebony wings outspread glided in ample circles over something dead below. The rock walls could not be climbed, and there seemed to be no passage across. At that moment Rydl, who had lagged behind, joined Zan. For the first time Rydl seemed to know where he was. "It is the cleft of the goddess," he said with a tone of fear and respect. "This place is sacred. Bad people are thrown here, and traitors. They fall so far that none hear them land." His eyes looked wild, and the wind blew in his hair.

Sacred or not, it had to be traversed, but that seemed to present no problem to Rydl. There was a place, he said, where the chasm narrowed and where passage was possible. Zan could see the narrowing section once it was pointed out to him. Rydl said that he had been there once with his father, but was never allowed across himself—until he ran away and crossed it without permission. Invading wasp men used this passage, Zan surmised, when their warriors pressed into his land and fell upon his kinsmen.

Zan was surprised to find in this leafless region a dead tree trunk stretched over the narrowest part of the gulf. It must have been dragged from some distance. Long since stripped of its bark, its silvered wood was gnarled and sinuous as dried meat, its fibers visible and distinct. The branches of this giant were mostly broken off, but bare stumps of them remained as handles to steady the traveler against the wind and the disabling terror of the height. Rydl went first, almost dancing across with the careless ease of childhood. Zan reflected that the boy was too stupid to be afraid. He tossed his spear to the other side and ventured with extreme caution, testing the steadiness of the log with a shift of his weight. Then holding on for dear life and never releasing one branch until another was in his hand, he ventured out. A quick, giddy glance below reminded him what was at stake. Then he looked no more. The last few steps had no branch to hold onto, and he had to trust to his sense of balance and a nimble final leap. Once across, Zan picked up his spear and looked back at the arid region he had traveled. Then he turned toward his destination. Rydl, who now could have led, followed behind as before.

Zan did not notice the changes in the terrain until his feet began to hurt. The land was becoming rocky, and soon he could see the projection of round, red boulders breaking the surface of the soil. After an hour's walk, rough trees began to reappear, but they were little more than scruffy bushes with dying, gnarled trunks. The rocks became larger and closer together, so that the two boys could almost walk from one rock to another; until with time they rose in sheer verticals over their heads and took on fantastic shapes and forms. This was the land of red rocks that Aniah had spoken of. As the travelers wandered into the region, which was fenced on two sides by high red cliffs, Zan thought he had never seen anything so wonderful and strange. Huge boulders, shattered from the sides of the rocky walls by the shaking earth, were scattered like giant toys and lay in crimson heaps. Some were smooth, some craggy and sharp. Some were round and others were squarish slabs cleaved from the face of the red cliff when once the ground had trembled. Ten strong men could not hope to lift the smallest of them.

Horizontal crevices marked the side of the cliff like deep wrinkles on an ancient face; while opposite, the might of nature had tipped the entire mountain on its side to reveal its inner workings. The titanic force had split the earth and sent its layers exploding upward or splaying downward according to its mood. There were time-eaten pillars absurdly balancing large boulders that ever threatened to fall if once disturbed by so much as a gust of wind. Zan wondered aloud what invisible hand had shaped these deadly marvels, but Rydl, jumping sportively from rock to rock and testing with playful shouts the echo that he had discovered, did not hear him.

The two walls of stone, immense and silent, between which the valley was situated, barred any escape. In the distance before them they could see a row of blue hills miles away. Rydl, who was wandering this way and that, luckily came upon a thin stream of water in the otherwise parched land. As the boys progressed, the cliff on their side curved inward, revealing a number of cave-like pockets dotting the red wall. Zan and Rydl climbed to several that were within reach before they found one that would make a good shelter. It was accessible and yet elevated some from the floor of the canyon, so that they could observe, unseen, any danger that might appear. In this empty vale, where every footstep seemed to produce an echo, they had not encountered a single soul, but that did not mean that no one was there. Zan was glad he had Rydl with him, for he had never seen a place so lonely, but he wished the child would be more cautious and not so noisy. Best to remain quiet and hidden as much as possible.

The cavelike dugout in which they settled was only three or four strides deep, and hardly high enough to stand up in, but of the several they had explored it was the best. Rydl soon discovered a store of nuts and seeds kept in a deep man-made indentation in the stone floor. Zan noticed some secret signs scratched into the wall directly above it. These things meant that people came, or once had come to this spot, and that the two boys could not stay for long without risking an encounter. Yet who knew how long these signs of life had been there unvisited? Dryness had preserved the grain and protected the carved marks—perhaps for many years.

They built a fire and made themselves comfortable. The sky was clear now and the sun beat down forcefully, but the dugout was shaded and cool. Food was at hand, and soon there might be more. Zan's feet were beginning to bleed, which was no small matter to a traveler. He was many days walk from home, and was quite possibly threatened by enemies. He could not easily run from them, and was still an uncertain distance from the dwellings of the wasp people. He decided to make this shelter a temporary resting place, to heal the scratches and blisters received in his long trek, and to restore his strength before he was completely exhausted.

Zan was glad to have time to think, to reflect on the high red cliffs and the fantastic stone giants towering over him. Wind-worn and strangely sculpted, they took on grotesque shapes which were sometimes almost human or animal. But just across, where the wall of the cliff turned to face him diagonally, was a shape that Zan thought ugly and unlucky. The collection of pits and dugouts confronting him took on the form of a skull. There was no mistaking it. It seemed to declare that Zan had wandered into a place of death, that he and his companion would perish there to be eaten by wolves or vultures, or be the prey of ants. Or perhaps he would find the remains of his twin nearby—Dael's withered corpse in the reddish dust. Zan lived in a superstitious time. He knew what a human skull looked like and what it meant. He stared at it from his shelter and contemplated it like a hermit in the desert. And as he gazed, almost transfixed and lost in foreboding, *something moved*—he didn't know what—within one of its hollow, dark eyes!

Jarred out of his reverie, he froze and whispered to Rydl to do the same. The sun would soon be down and both of the boys watched minutely for any further motion. Best to know at once what enemies they would have to deal with. It was five silent minutes before they saw what it was. A bobcat was noiselessly emerging from its den. This was a night hunter readying himself as dusk approached. It was not very large as the great cats go, but it was a fierce and dangerous animal. It had a short tail and points of hair on the tips of its ears. Its beautiful fur was spotted and grew thick on the sides of its face. With an athletic bound and graceful, experienced steps it made its way to a large rock and perched on top of it. It had seen some partridges nearby and so it waited, waited for their return.

From their higher position, Zan and Rydl could observe the entire drama—how the bobcat watched patiently until two partridges came into view below, how it stared at them with a fixed and intense glare while, as it prepared to spring, its tail twitched nervously. With similar fixity the boys watched the watcher as it crept ever closer, its hindquarters rising in anticipation. Then, in a moment, it had a crushed partridge under each paw.

"Quick, Rydl, let us take the birds for ourselves!" Rydl hesitated, for the cat might well have killed him too. "Follow me with your stick, and scream and strike when I do."

It was not a matter calling for stealth. With a sudden rush and a loud scream Zan charged directly at the cat, striking it on its tender nose with his spear. The startled bobcat, which was at least as hungry as Zan, hissed and sprang away as if it had stepped on hot coals, releasing the partridges in spite of itself. Zan continued without cease to assault its nose and eyes, and when Rydl joined in the attack it saw itself outnumbered and withdrew, abandoning any inclination to fight for its prey. The boys seized the birds for themselves. "You see, Rydl, although the cat had speed and ferocity on its side, courage and surprise won out. Now, let us feast." Zan did not see it, but Rydl gazed at him with admiration and affection.

As they turned toward their shelter, Zan noticed for the first time that the rocks and gaps around his cave also formed a skull. He and Rydl had been in death's mouth this whole time! He thought about it and laughed to himself. "Two skulls. Not one. Two." It meant nothing!

They built a fire at the edge of the dugout and cleaned and roasted the birds. Tearing them apart with no nicety, they ate their fill while joking and laughing at the bobcat, which had been outfaced from its prize and was probably nearby smelling the aroma and wishing it could join in the feast. The good food and good humor made Zan feel less like an enclosed animal and more like a man—and a man very much alive! He wished that his father and uncle had been there when he had robbed the cat of its prey, for it was they who had taught him this trick. "Even large cats can be cowards at times," Thal had said. (That was even before Zan had killed the lion.) "We do not run from animals," he had said laughing. "We eat them!" Zan wondered what they were doing at that moment, so many miles away. Thal was probably working away on a tool or weapon, and Chul might be hunting mushrooms, or else snoring after supper.

A change of weather brought Zan back to himself. It was quite suddenly cooler, and the force of the wind increased. Far off, in the direction of the blue hills the sky was turning black, although it was still clear overhead. Brilliant, jagged flashes of lightning were visible in the darkening distance, with a rumble of thunder following each flash. Still far off, the black cloud began to shed its store in a veil of water. Fascinated and glad, Zan watched the sheet of rain approach closer and closer, bringing ever brighter lightning and amazing explosions of thunder with the renewing wetness. Everything could be observed from the safe, dry dugout, but Rydl, overwhelmed by the violence of the storm, clung firmly to Zan, his eyes rolling in terror. Then the storm passed as it had come, the menacing winds brushing against their faces for a while after. "We are safe here, Rydl. Let us sleep."

When the two boys rose the next day, their entire surroundings had changed. The sky was clear and blue again, but the downpour had brought out the redness of the land. Everything—rocks, earth, even water—was tinged. Only the dark green shrubs, that seemed always to be in a struggle to survive, provided contrast, washed and refreshed by the rain. Crimson cascades poured from the tops of the cliffs, and the tiny stream they had discovered the day before had swelled into a driving crimson river, crashing and churning over obstructing rocks. But by afternoon the power had gone out of the water, and after three days the river was reduced to the same paltry stream that it had been when they first came. Then another downpour appeared, almost identical to the other—distinct from afar and visibly arriving on the wind. Sheets of water sent Zan and Rydl to their hollow, where they looked aghast on the ribs of lightning, and then observed the transformation a sudden shower made on the sun-parched soil. A while afterwards, the setting sun gleamed on the freshly wet land, and its ardent glow made their red world redder.

After a week of rest and healing, it was time to leave this place of shelter. Rydl, delighted to be on the move again, skipped after Zan like a small animal, familiar with every rock and foothold and playing among the stones. A chipmunk drank from a dent in a boulder where water had gathered, and Rydl tried to catch it. Failing, he returned to the natural basin and drank from the same pool, and so did Zan.

On the second day they came to a place where the passage between the two cliffs was partially blocked off by a huge stone arch which bridged most of the canyon. A challenging climb would allow the boys to see beyond it, so they mounted boulder after boulder until they reached the opening. Wind blew through it, and they paused to recover their strength and to survey the new view. The strong but refreshing breeze cooled them from their laborious ascent—the reward for their efforts. A greater reward was the vista that opened before them. They still saw the red land and ragged brush, but in the far distance, quite visible now, lay the range of blue hills; and still farther were mountains that rose so high that they seemed to blend with the sky and become as immaterial as the air itself. "My motherland is there," Rydl said, and he pointed to a pair of round and softly shaded hills that stood somewhat apart from the others. "Then we will go there," Zan said.

7 THE WASP PEOPLE

A mountain is always much farther away than it looks. The two boys walked until they were weary, and yet the hills seemed no closer than when they started. Whole days went by and the land gradually rose, gradually changed from red spotted with green to green only occasionally spotted with red. Long uphill travel brought about this transformation, during which time Zan and Rydl had the usual problems of finding food and shelter. Zan was able to bring down another rabbit with his sling, to the wonder of Rydl, who tried the weapon but became bored with it when he was unable to control it. Then, when halfway up one of the hills, Zan saw something on the other hill that made him look again. Standing on a large, naked rock and silhouetted against the sky was a sight that overwhelmed Zan with joy. It was Dael!

"Dael, it's me! It's Zan," he yelled, and rushed toward the place. Dael did not respond at all, but stood as if he had turned to stone. Zan rushed breathlessly toward him and called again, his young friend lagging well behind.

Only the echo responded. For a time Zan lost sight of him. Then he reappeared and Zan called out yet again. After a quarter of an hour Zan suspected the truth, and as he came closer finally accepted that what he had seen was but a tower of stone, the topmost formation resembling Dael's globe of hair which was always recognizable from a distance. It looked like Dael. It looked like Zan himself. But it was only a bitter disappointment. Yet the incident was fortunate, for as he resumed his upward path he came to a ridge beyond which was a wonderful, unexpected vision.

What had been completely hidden from view until he had reached the top of the ridge was a lake, crystal, pure and beautiful as any dream. It was surrounded by lush trees, many of which, as in a garden, bloomed rose, snow white, and lilac, so that the air was fragrant with their nectar. Green with sap, a weeping willow bent its luminous branches toward the water to be reflected in its stillness; and a deer drank peacefully in the distance, unaware or unconcerned with Zan's presence. Halfway across, populated by a cluster of young white birches, was a small island at the shore of which stood a slender and statuesque white egret. Moving with natural elegance, the bird suddenly rose in wonderfully graceful flight, its broad, black-tipped wings low and silent over the water, which gave back the gliding reflection. Rising high over this fair haven was a granite cliff, still sunny. Its stone, pink in the light and violet in the shade, reflected on the fractured surface of the water with gorgeous multiplicity. From the top, a stream of water plunged fifty feet to strike the far side of the lake with thundering commotion—although the sound came softly to Zan's ears, for it was some distance away. Zan did not so much hear the waterfall as see the sun's glint upon it, and the glorious arched rainbow generated by the mist—raised when water pummels rock and dashes into spume.

Zan had never seen a place so lovely. Indeed, it was the first time in his young life that he was even aware that the world he lived in *could* be lovely. For him nature was harsh and threatening—an enemy to struggle against and survive within. How different it seemed now! He thought he might live happily forever in this beautiful, peaceful refuge. Soon the trees would be heavy with fruit, and in the meantime he could eat the blossoms. He could see fish in the clear water, and still the deer drank and grazed in the distance. "Rydl! Look! Rydl!" he called, and the doe looked up with ears outspread. A bright red bird, startled by his voice, flitted across his vision. "Rydl, where are you?" But Rydl, as Zan soon realized, was gone.

"He will be back," Zan thought. "He is probably wandering and exploring." Rydl was a lad who could not stay still for a moment. Instead of searching for him, Zan decided to take a swim. It had been a hot day, and the clear blue water invited him. How delicious it was to plunge under the surface! Below and clearly visible, green growth rose toward him and the fish gaped in wonder. He could not hope to catch anything while swimming, but he noticed a number of holes on the bottom where the water was shallower and the plants did not obscure his view. There he waded waist deep, and looking carefully at a hole on the muddy floor, submerged his head and thrust his hand into the opening. He was not at all surprised, and was quite ready, when the sizable jaws of a catfish clamped down on his whole hand! No doubt laying eggs under the water, the infuriated fish was defending its haunt with instinctive ferocity. Zan pulled his hand back, fish and all, and held it thrashing between his legs until he could grasp it by the gill with his other hand. Then with some effort he dragged it toward the shore while it beat against the water with all its might. Zan put it on the ground where it helplessly panted and pounded its tail for a while. It was almost as large as Zan's thigh, an ugly, whiskered creature, with bulging eyes. Zan examined his hand to see how much damage the fish's jaws had done. A little blood, that was all. Thal had taught Zan to catch fish in this way, and Zan was very good at it, but this was the largest either he or his father had ever landed. At this lake he could catch one every day if he liked! He cleaned it and began to build a fire.

"Fear the spirits most when they are excessively kind." Zan never got to taste his fish. As he was bending down to blow on the tinder, his hands and knees on the ground and his face low, he looked up for a moment and saw a number of legs around him. He had been encircled by fierce, spear-bearing warriors! Forgetting his fire and his fish, Zan rose to face them. They were a strong and manly people, not slender like his own, but healthy, tall, and full-fleshed. It was plain that they ate well. Their strong limbs were decorated with swirling designs, but what was most strange was that they had bright red swirls painted around their eyes, which made them appear ferocious and magical. Every man held a spear, and each spear was tipped with a sharp blade on which there was a reddish substance. Zan knew instantly that these were the wasp people with their poisoned spears. He had found his destination—or it had found him!

"Why are you here?" one of them said in the foreign, grumbling voice that Zan only barely understood. Zan began to reply, but none of the men could tell what he was saying, so they just went on talking without regarding him: "We sold you to the Noi and told you to stay with them. You do not belong here. Why do you return?"

Were they crazy? They were acting as if they knew him—and suddenly Zan realized that they thought he was Dael! It was Dael they had sold and sent away to the Noi, whoever they were. Never did Zan have to think more quickly! He had first to stay alive, then to find out who and where these Noi were, and finally to make his escape in order to recover Dael—if Dael were still alive. Clever speech would be no good to him now, and in a moment of invention Zan decided to take the opposite course. He would be *stupid*. He would garble his speech in order to make himself even more difficult to understand. He would look at his feet, shuffle, and scratch. He would mumble to himself. And he would pretend that he could understand nothing at all, let alone their language. Apparently they did not remember much of Dael, and who knew but that they considered Dael a fool too since he could not speak as they did.

The wasp men took his fish for themselves, tying Zan up and thumping him along with the butt end of their spears. They made no more attempt to communicate with the "idiot," and brought Zan to their camp. His spear and bag were taken too, as prizes, but luckily he had his sling wrapped around his waist, and no one suspected that it was a weapon. Zan deliberately twitched as he walked, mumbling audibly. Then he saw Rydl lagging behind. It was he who had betrayed him to them, had shown them where he was. Zan thought of telling the wasp men that he had brought Rydl back to them, but he soon saw that they considered him to be Rydl's kidnapper, and he decided to remain silent according to his plan.

Zan held one advantage over his captors. He could understand their speech and they did not know it. Moreover, by pretending to be foolish he might cause them to be careless about him. Rydl had not told his people much, nor did they seem inclined to listen to a mere child.

When they arrived at their camp, Zan observed with wonder the way they lived. Arranged in a circle were some bulbous shelters shaped of twigs, bark, and mud daubing—just as Aniah had described them. But looking up, Zan realized that most of their round, hollow dwellings were suspended in the trees, high above the ground. These structures looked like, and evidently were inspired by wasps' nests, especially as each was entered through a round hole just large enough to admit one man. Excellent climbers, the wasp people were as much at home in the trees as on the ground. They could suddenly leap or swing onto any intruder—or they could retreat into their hives for defense. Zan soon grasped how warlike these people were. No man went anywhere without a spear in his hand, and always it was tipped with a poisoned blade.

In time Zan learned more, for it was his fate to spend many months with them. The men spent a good deal of their time in councils of war or, dressed as wasps, in grotesque rituals to prepare themselves for battle. In these they danced and chanted in unison: *Ah ah UH! Ah ah UH!* They emitted a loud, warlike buzzing sound and brandished their red-tipped spears, so that in a single line, as in a dance, every man raised his weapon with the same hand, at the same angle, and at the same time. The impression was not so much of many men as of one giant, poisonous, hissing centipede.

Zan soon understood that there were other wasp-clans, and that they were constantly at war with each other. Indeed, they were almost at war with themselves! They were a quarrelsome and boastful people, ready to fight over any supposed insult, bent on conquest and preoccupied with revenge. As with his own people, the clans never intermarried, each one considering any such connection with the others to be debasing and dishonorable. Volatile and extreme in their natures, they were one day on their faces in terror of their gods, and the next day blaspheming them, stealing, and even committing murder—overwhelmed with dark and destructive passions. Gradually Zan discovered the nature of these wildmen, and pondered in his heart how he and his own tribesmen might use his newfound knowledge of their old enemies.

When Zan was first taken captive he was immediately bound, his arms cruelly tied to a pole behind his back. He was put in the charge of a youth named Naz. Zan grew to hate this fellow more than he had ever hated anyone in his life. Naz was tall, muscular, and almost a grown man. He had hair of a strange yellow color like dried grass, which spilled in softer growth down his cheeks. His deeply set blue eyes were his most handsome feature, but they maintained that cruel squint which lets in what it wants to see and keeps out the rest. He looked on Zan with a steely glance. Zan was smaller than him, appeared to be unable to speak, and seemed mentally afflicted too. Right away Naz conceived a supercilious contempt for Zan-Gah. He prodded him with unnecessary roughness, and when he discovered Zan's scars he could only ask with scorn whether the girls had scratched him. Rather than replying, Zan bent abjectly and rolled his eyes, letting his tongue escape from his mouth as if there were something seriously wrong with him. Words of scorn had hardly come to Naz's lips when he received from Zan-Gah a swift kick in the groin which left him moaning on the ground. Zan resumed his pretense of foolishness and the other men laughed uproariously, a couple of them giving Naz an additional kick in the backside, while the girls present tittered. Naz was a good-looking young man (as he well knew), and used to female admiration. Ordinarily they would laugh at his every word, and laughed now too. Naz could not forget his humiliation, and in future days never missed an opportunity to afflict the stranger boy in his keeping.

Zan was put to work within a hut that was used by the women, while Naz kept guard outside. Because Zan made no attempt to escape, and seemed dull of mind, the

strictness of his guard soon was relaxed. Naz was bored
with his assignment, either taking his displeasure out on
Zan or ignoring his duty altogether. Yet Zan postponed
flight because he knew that there was much to be learned
from his enemies. In the watch of the women if not of
Naz, he was considered to be safely in keep, working
on their chores. He was made to build and attend fires,
to grind and boil seeds or shell nuts, and to otherwise
prepare food. He cleaned and roasted game, and softened
the skins by chewing them. Any unpleasant task was apt
to be given to him.

As with his own people, there was a distinct line
between the work of men and women, and as with
his own, there was deep shame in crossing the well-
established separation. Zan had always held the labor of
women in high respect, necessary and gratefully received
by everybody; yet his tribesmen would no sooner do
it themselves than seek to bear a child, which was the
special gift of women. Among the wasp people too, it was
well understood that Zan was humbled as much as one
of his feeble intelligence could be. In their eyes he was
both weak of mind and deprived of any masculinity, and
therefore lacking in the least dignity. Eventually, however,
it was recalled that "the idiot" was a good fisherman, so
he was permitted to go to the lake sometimes, under
Naz's unpleasant guard. Zan was the one who was made
to gut the fish, whoever caught them, using a flint blade
which was always taken from him when he was done.

Zan accepted in silence the humiliation put upon
him; he was not as ready to take abuse from Naz. But

dull and stupid as Zan pretended to be, he noticed that Naz avoided coming very close to him. Naz had learned that lesson! One time, indeed, Naz had poked him in the thigh with the point of his spear, more for fun than for any reason. The point had barely penetrated his skin, but the wound was as painful and disabling as a serpent's sting. It both hurt and deadened, so that Zan could hardly move his leg. Naz gleefully watched as Zan groaned and stumbled, thrusting the poisoned spear repeatedly in Zan's direction as if to wound him yet again. The women came to protect Zan, as often they had before, sharply reproving Naz for taking advantage of a feeble-minded child. The venom hurt terribly for about half an hour, then gradually wore off, leaving its victim as he had been before. Now, for what it was worth, Zan had a pretty good idea of the nature of this weapon. In hunting, the venom itself did not kill the deer, but rather incapacitated it so that it could be taken even if it was only slightly wounded. Zan longed to learn the secret of this potion, and bided his time that he might. The poison was used exclusively by the males of the tribe, but its preparation was in the hands of the women. And soon it was in his hands too, for he was ordered one day to grind the berries from which it was made. Later on he got to accompany the women gatherers. It was a small, inedible red berry which he had often seen in his own region, although no one at home had guessed its value. With this knowledge the clans could stand up to the wasp people or any invader, and could bring down game more easily too.

After a while Naz was relieved of the duty (which he much resented) of guarding "the idiot." A woman named

Hurnoa, who disliked any disorder or nonsense, spoke out with her characteristic firmness in Zan's defense. Perhaps she foresaw that he and Naz would end by killing one another if left in each other's presence for long. Anyway, all but Naz had grown tired of humiliating him. It had been settled for good that Zan was stupid and incapable of doing real harm, so he was largely ignored. Still Zan awaited the right moment, allowing chances of escape to pass. He had a degree of freedom but did not yet use it to get away.

Zan did make preparations, however. He began hiding things—a blade, a supply of dry food, and a spear which he had taken when no one was watching. Zan's strategy had been a success. He had put his enemies to sleep by acting dull and harmless, and now he could get away with a good deal. When things were missed, no one suspected him of taking them. He had even spirited away a supply of the wasp men's poison for future use! He had managed to hide some items outside of the village by a large rock near his fishing site, but the spear and poison he kept at hand under his bedding. Meanwhile he still had his sling wrapped around his waist, and no one noticed or cared. All of this prudent care and stealth did him no good, however.

Zan stayed with his enemies for over a year. He knew their language thoroughly, although he would not speak more than a word or two lest he lose his reputation for stupidity. He could learn nothing of the Noi, who held Dael, and dared not ask, although it was crucial knowledge if he were to find his brother. Then one day, when he knew he must soon flee without the information he sought, he heard the elders talking excitedly about him. Moving as close as he could, he understood the anger of their words more than the words themselves, which were out of earshot. He sensed a new peril, for he knew that things had not been going well for the wasp people. Food had become scarce, as he could clearly see from his own decreased rations. The rains had stopped and the lake was drying around its margins where he had formerly been able to take fish at will. Worse, a strange sickness was spreading among them and several people had died. The chiefs, unable to account for the series of disasters, conceived the superstitious idea that "the idiot" had brought them bad luck. Thanks to Zan's fakery, his very glance now seemed baleful and unwholesome. Zan could barely hear what was being said, but he heard enough to realize that he was in danger.

The next morning, even as Zan was planning his escape, they came for him. With the sort of roughness he had not suffered for some time they prodded him along to a high place on a mountainside. It took most of the day to get there. Zan looked for an opportunity to run, but he was surrounded by several armed men. Remembering what Rydl had told him, that prisoners were hurled to their deaths, Zan wondered with fear whether they intended to slay him in this same terrible way. They were taking him higher and higher for no apparent reason. Then, looking around for any escape at all, he spied Rydl trailing behind. Rydl was avoiding being seen by dodging from one rock or tree to another, peeking out as if he were playing one of his games. What did he want, who had so long ignored his existence—to witness his murder?

At length the group came to a crest roughly situated between two mountains, where a hot wind blew on them. As they rose to its brink, Zan felt sure that his time had come, and got ready to resist and flee. A sudden break away and he was running with all his might toward the woods with six tall men charging after him. Zan did not get far. The men split into two groups which flanked him on either side like a hunted deer, and swift of foot soon had him in hand, dragging him back to the crest. Zan prepared to die. He gazed in terror over the edge—but there was no cliff or deep pit at all. An entirely new scene opened before him. As far as his eyes could see there lay a gray and yellowish sickly land, ragged with rocks and scruffy brush. He turned his head around toward his captors and saw behind him the wasp men's land of stately trees, water, and lush growth. He looked the other way again. There he saw not his death, but a dismal land of death. The mountains, like a great natural fence, made a sharp divide between two strikingly different landscapes, one green and one dry.

"Go!" the gruesomely painted leader said, still sweating after his run, so that the red swirls dripped like blood around his eyes. "Go, and bring us no more misfortune. *There* is where we sent you," and he pointed to the desert. "That is your land. This is ours. Do not come back again or we will surely kill you." One of the men gave him a final kick which Zan did not return. He advanced toward the parched land below, assured that Dael had been sent there and secretly wishing to go there to seek him. The wasp men, with a final gesture of wrath and anathema, turned to go home.

No sooner had the wasp men left than Rydl came out of hiding, calling to him softly while carefully observing their departure. Rydl had somehow gotten hold of Zan's possessions, saving them for a whole year. The spear with which Zan had killed the lion was there, along with his sack and some food Rydl had placed inside. Zan found the goat skin, the fire-making kit, and even the black blade that Chul had given him. Most important, his hollow gourd canteen was there, filled with water. "I have kept these for you, Zan, and have kept your secrets too. I knew you were no fool, but I never said so." Rydl had grown during the year of Zan's captivity, both in height and in maturity.

"I thank you, Rydl, and will always remember you as a friend when I most needed one." Rydl hugged Zan-Gah and they said goodbye.

8 THE LAND OF DEATH

As Zan descended he remembered well what Aniah had told him: "Do not go where none can live." But what choice had he? Dael was out there somewhere, sold to the Noi and probably made a slave, as he himself had been for the last year. Zan hoped it was so for he still clung to the belief that his brother was alive. The wasp warriors who had driven him away had pointed a little to the right rather than straight ahead, and Zan took that to be his proper direction. For all the barrenness of the land, he saw at some distance in the blazing region a meandering path of greenery, which told him that a stream might be found there. He had not gone far when he came across a flat, vertical slab of stone which had a curious emblem scratched into its surface. Zan examined the design with curiosity. It consisted of a wild-eyed woman flanked on either side by two men raising their spears. Perhaps she was a goddess or a demon. No doubt she and her attendants were meant to warn off intruders, but Zan was not much frightened by these geometric figures. At least they indicated that people sometimes came there without dying of thirst!

The sun was high in the sky and the rocks underfoot were hot, but there was nothing to do except endure it until he could get to the stream, which was a good distance away. Zan had time to think even as he walked on the burning surface. This part of the journey would prove to be the most difficult of all his trials. He had to provide himself with food, water, and shelter in this hostile wasteland! The fierce sun told him that he needed shelter right away. Already it was drying his throat and burning his skin. He took the animal pelt still packed in his sack and covered his head and shoulders as best he could. Lucky that Rydl had saved it for him! But the deeper he went into this sun-baked and desolate place, the more frightened he became. "Always face your enemy," his father had taught him, but this enemy was neither before nor behind him. It was everywhere—in front and behind, over and under! Zan wondered once again whether he was going to die. Panic seized his heart and his breath almost left him. He stopped in his dusty tracks, looked around, and said aloud, "I will not panic!" and even forced himself to smile at his situation. Immediately he felt a bit better. "If this is a land of death, how can so many things be alive?" Zan observed the cactuses that had begun to appear in great numbers. Endless in variety, they were flowering vigorously in purple, orange, and lemon. At almost every step a lizard or rodent darted out of his path. He had to dodge the scorpions. Overhead an eagle soared, and other birds also flew in the bright and cloudless sky. This desert place was actually teeming with life! All of these creatures could survive and thrive! Why shouldn't Zan-Gah? A ball of tumbleweed blew across his path, dead as anything could be. "That too was alive not long ago.

I must try to learn the secrets of things that live—to become part of the desert instead of struggling against it!" In this way Zan tried to encourage himself and keep his presence of mind.

It was not long before Zan discovered that certain succulent plants (the likes of which he had never seen before) were full of liquid. He knew better than to suck their juices, however, because many plants were poisonous—just as the berries were that the wasp women used to make their venom. Fortunately Zan still had some water, but he wanted to conserve it as long as he could. He rubbed some of the sap—not much—inside of his lower lip, as Thal once had taught him. If his lip swelled or became sore he would know not to swallow any more of it. Zan applied very little at first, knowing that some plants are deadly, even in small quantities. A little later, if he suffered no bad effects, he would try a somewhat larger amount. At length Zan successfully tested three different desert plants that provided moisture, and food too. One of them, a cactus, was so round and bulbous that Zan was fairly certain it stored quantities of liquid. He broke it open with a large rock, but the pieces were covered with needles, which made them hard to handle. Another cactus plant was sweet to the taste, both its sap and its flesh, but it too was covered with spiky thorns. Zan was out of water when he arrived at the creek, and to his bitter disappointment, all he found was a dry riverbed. It had looked better from a distance.

For all his efforts and discoveries, Zan was parched and famished. He found himself eating bugs and a lizard, knowing that he could not continue this way for very long. He needed water. He noticed the paw prints of an animal in the dust, and then others, small and large, mostly going the same way. Zan followed them to a puddle in the rocky bottom of the creek that he had not seen. It was all that was left of what had once been a stream. Something scampered away and Zan lay down to drink what was left. He managed to refill his canteen, and decided to settle for a while. The bank of the creek gave him some shade and the few sickly trees that clung to it provided the materials for a basic lean-to shelter.

The thought of advancing further into the harsh, dry land was hateful to him. He needed rest badly and considered traveling by night when it would be cooler. Building a fire was unusually easy because everything was so dry, and Zan was glad he had done so when he felt how cold the desert was at night. He thought of the heavy lion skin he had left with Chul, and he wished that he had it. It was soon time to go, but he could hardly see a thing, so he waited for dawn. Waited....

When Zan awoke the day was well advanced. He looked for his puddle of water but it had dried in the sun. However, the river bed was still a little soft and taking his spear, he poked it into the ground where the water had been. The hole filled, and with a little more digging, Zan had a supply of filthy, brackish water. It would not last, and as things were going, neither would he! Who knew how far he had to go? Nor was he sure that he was even moving in the right direction. Zan decided not to wait for evening. At some distance he saw a high buildup of rocky layers that would be worth climbing if only his strength held out. From its top he could survey the area and see where he wanted to go.

Zan did not reach the hillock until afternoon. He paused for a while to rest, and became aware that two coyotes were following him. Zan would not have paid much attention to one animal, but two worried him. He took his sling from his waist and gathered some rocks. Zan had managed to keep the sling for a whole year without once using it. It was time to try it out. Pelting the animals with stones, but missing his targets again and again, he began to get the feel of the weapon once more, and finally succeeded in driving them off with pained yelps. But Zan sensed that his strength was failing him. He still had a steep climb ahead, and pressed on until he achieved the summit exhausted. His whole body, and especially his hands and feet ached and stung. He lay flat on his back and looked at the blanched sky while he caught his breath.

At length Zan rose and looked around in a wide circle. The hills lay behind him, the declining sun still glowing on their granite tops. Before him lay the same field of stone, sand, and cactus for as far as the eye could see. But at the very limit of his vision he noticed a gleaming silver surface that could only be a lake reflecting the white-hot sky. And the lake beckoned to him.

Zan was dying. A week had passed during which he had walked both day and night. He no longer had the energy to hunt nor even to build a fire. He had used up his store of water, and the relief of morning dew or cactus juice simply was not enough. Jackrabbits sometimes appeared with their large, fanlike ears, but Zan was no longer able to hunt them. He remembered the weak and starving Hru and realized that he was in their situation, only worse! They at least had water. He tried to ignore the miserable emptiness of his stomach but he could not ignore his thirst. If he managed to catch a lizard he ate it as it was, needing its moisture more than its nourishment. To cook it (had he the strength left to build a fire) would only have dried it out. He found some small eggs that would keep him alive for another day, and ate them ravenously, shells and all.

Zan began to stagger and to fall, so that his knees were scraped. And were black vulture wings soaring over his head? The blazing, relentless sun smote sorely on him, while the hot and ceaseless wind provided no relief at all. Heat-tortured, aching, and thirstier than he ever had been in his life, only one thing kept him going—the vision of the lake as he had seen it from the high rock, gleaming silver on the farthest horizon. Zan thought of its wetness all day and dreamed of it whenever he slept, waking with his head throbbing and his tongue stuck to the roof of his mouth. Only the lake, only the lake could save him!

Finally one day Zan gratefully caught a glimpse of its shiny face perhaps two miles off. Or was it ten? Distances were so hard to measure in this sun-baked expanse, and seemed always to be much greater than he had thought. Staggering, dizzy and nauseous, he approached it at last, unless it was in his imagination—a dream, or a hallucination brought on by starvation. The sand had become a white powder, and when Zan fell, for he could no longer keep his feet, it burned his scraped knees and the wounds and sores covering his body. Zan didn't care anymore. He was finished. When he finally reached the lake—which seemed to have taken forever—he had no more strength. He literally fell onto its gnat-covered surface and let the tepid water, filthy with insects, flow into his open mouth. To his grievous surprise it burned his cracked lips and throat, and seared his eyes. It was salt. *The water was heavy with salt!* Zan fainted away, bereft of any power. The last thing he saw was the skeleton of an unrecognizable animal.

9 CHUL

Each of us is a little different from anyone else, but Chul was much different. From his birth, his strangeness declared itself. He came from his gasping mother unusually large, red, wrinkled, and covered with hair like a baby ape. He howled in an unusually loud voice for a baby, and his face twisted as he cried. When the women showed the squalling newborn to his father, Bray, he looked at the creature and frowned so that his face was twisted too. Father and son, squinting and grimacing at each other, looked comically alike for a moment. Bray gave his new son the name Chul, which in fact meant Ape.

Poor Chul! All of his life people laughed at him. He was an ugly child. His eyes were too close together and his lower lip hung down stupidly over his almost nonexistent chin. His posture was never erect except when he rose to sniff the air for danger—or to whiff an animal roasting on a spit. To make matters worse, his nose had been broken early in life and twisted to one side. Add that he was thick of speech, spoke but little in his rumbling voice, and that he was as big as his father by the time he was nine years old. Growing up, he had a monstrous appetite, and for a time he was not allowed to eat until the others had gotten their share lest he eat everything! Yes, he was big for his age! What did he not shovel into his mouth whenever he could?

Chul's comrades made fun of his size and awkwardness, and called him stupid to his face. Chul only laughed along with them, until one older youth made the mistake of throwing a stone at him. Lout that he was, Chul was not too stupid to resent this obvious insult, and the smile vanished from his face. Seizing the foolish lad, Chul lifted him over his head and threw him about ten feet. It was fortunate for the youth that he landed in a soft mud puddle instead of on the hard rocks, but even so he was sufficiently hurt. Then the "ape" was sorry he had injured him, and later they made friends. It was not in Chul's easygoing nature to bear grudges.

If ever a man was a hodgepodge, it was Chul. He was a strange and preposterous mixture of good and bad, but on the whole his goodness was dominant. As is often the case with unattractive people, Chul had concealed virtues: a generous heart, courage, fierce loyalty, and sometimes insight. The time was coming when his clan would be grateful for these qualities—as well as for his physical might.

Chul's strength was legendary before he was a man. He once wrenched by the horns a young bull too frisky for three men to subdue, breaking its neck with a loud crack, so that the entire clan could feast on its carcass like a pride of lions. It was said that Chul could wrestle down a stag single-handed if he could only catch one—and eat it single-handed too! Fortunately he learned early to share, and in time came to be known for his generosity as well as his enormous appetite. He began losing the hair on his head before he was twenty, and some of his teeth soon thereafter. By that time the war among the five clans had begun again, ending a long period of quiet. Often the object of mockery, Chul would prove his value in the renewed fighting.

He took a leading part. Standing at least a head taller than his fellows, the very sight of Chul with a troop of warriors, or the mere sound of his wild battle cry, could rout an enemy troop of even greater size. He preferred the club to the spear, and had one that reached to his brother's chest. It was a gnarled staff of hardwood that twisted and turned up to the great, spiky knob. Woe to the man who was struck with it! He would be unlikely to recover from the blow! Sometimes Chul chose to use the spear instead of this rude bludgeon. His spear was thick and heavy enough to support the roof of a shelter! No one would want these weapons. They were too large to use, yet Chul wielded them with ease and with terrible effectiveness.

In battle Chul had another advantage. He seemed almost impervious to wounds. A blow that might have been fatal to most men he returned again with deadly results. Once, when he received a serious hurt in the thigh, he went on hollering and fighting, and only drew out the spear embedded in his leg after his enemies had fled.

Soon after he killed the kinsman of Aniah, something happened in his mind. He had had enough of killing, and regretted the way he had ambushed the man without warning. From that time onward he refused to go looking for the enemy, and was only willing to fight if his foes came to him. The other men of the clan were less disposed to go on the offensive without their giant, and the conflict seemed to have burned itself out. In fact, it came to a stop for several years.

The invasion of the wasp men brought the clans together. They had to put aside their feud for their very survival, and turn their attention to a new enemy. It was fortunate that the wasp warriors had not come against them in full strength. As Zan was to learn much later, the alien clans were often at odds with each other. Had they cooperated together, their combined might would have overwhelmed Zan's people before he and Dael were born. They had greater numbers and superior weaponry. Their poison spears did not need to kill to incapacitate, and even Chul, wounded slightly with a venomous point, was slowed down a bit—although he went right on fighting and bellowing his astonishing war-cry. Standing together, it had been possible to chase off the invaders. But that was an assault by only one of the several clans of wasp people. Perhaps one day they might return in greater numbers.

A period of peace followed, and Chul decided to get a wife. His feats on the field of battle would have recommended most men to the females of the clan; but it can be guessed how few of them wanted Chul for a husband! Luckily for him there was one. Her name was Siraka-Finaka, which referred to her small size. (Finaka means Wren's Nest.) Chul could not pronounce her name, so he called her Aka. Standing on her toes, her nose just reached to his navel! But if she was small in size, she was mighty in spirit. Those she could not control with her physique she would quickly bring to bay with her energetic and dominating personality.

Chul did not choose Siraka-Finaka; she chose him—and once she did, Chul knew that he might as well not try to escape the marriage bed she had planned for him. Eventually they had three daughters whom Chul loved with all of his brute heart. With the coming of children his character softened considerably, and he did not resent the laughter that followed him; for what could have been more ridiculous than this giant being held strictly in line by his tiny wife, or more odd than the hairy warrior melting into tenderness when he held his baby girls and made baby sounds? He adored them; and was terrified of displeasing Siraka-Finaka, for his dull tongue was no match for her sharp one. Mighty Chul, who feared nothing, feared his woman.

When Zan-Gah decided to seek his brother, Chul suggested timidly to his wife that it might help if he went along. Siraka-Finaka would have hit him in the head if she could have reached it! But if she did not strike him with her small fist, she struck him with her tongue, and kept on striking too! Chul, she reminded him, had a family to feed and protect; and Zan-Gah would have to find his twin by himself. Later the subject came up again—with the same unpleasant result, but after a year went by and Zan did not return, both Thal and Chul were much concerned, and Chul once again suggested to his wife that he should seek news of Zan-Gah. The great ape, Chul, and his tiny wren-wife could be heard roaring and chirping for a long time that night. Finally Chul, tongue-tied with rage, picked up his spear and stormed out. Here was this dwarfish woman, a third his size (if that), ruling the roost and telling him what he could or could not do! His younger brother, Thal, would not have stood for it, and neither would he!

10 THE CAVE

The first thing Zan sensed was the absence of torturing heat. His skin still burned and his head ached fearfully, as it had under the blistering sun, but now he was shivering with cold, and so weak that he could not rise from the bed of soft furs in which he found himself. In trying to get up Zan groaned aloud, and someone bent over him, a girl with an expression of anxiety furrowing her brow. Zan wanted to ask where he was and how he came there. He also wondered what new danger he was in, but from weakness more than stealth he waited and looked around. The dim light came from torches bracketed on what he realized were the uneven walls of a cave. He squinted, pretending to sleep, and glanced at the girl caring for him. As she bathed his forehead with cool water he opened his eyes wide and looked directly at her. Her hair, cascading to his shoulders, was of a fiery hue he had never seen before; and her eyes were the greenish color of something rare. So striking was her appearance that Zan thought she was a demon, but her soft, low voice and gentle manner showed that she was not.

"Dael," she said almost tenderly, "what has happened to you?" and tears trickled from her strange eyes down her freckled cheeks. Her language was almost the same as that of the wasp people, and Zan understood her perfectly.

Zan tried to speak and could not, but after she assisted him in sipping some warm broth he managed to croak out "I am not Dael."—to which she gasped out "Oh, Dael!" Zan, sick as he was, immediately recognized the problem. The girl mistook him for his twin. He fell back onto his bed and repeated in the same hoarse voice that he was not Dael, at length managing to add that Dael was his twin brother. The flame-headed girl stared at him with astonishment. He looked exactly like Dael. How could he be anybody else?

"Why do you tease me, Dael? You frighten me to death." Then as she scrutinized his half-naked body, she saw his scars and realized that this was indeed Dael's twin.

Twins were so unusual among her people that they were the objects of superstitious dread. Terribly affrighted, she leapt away, her back to the side of the cave, her green eyes nearly popping out of her head. Then, as if recalling herself, she straightened up and said, "I am a daughter of Noi, and of a people so ancient that some gods were not even born when we came here as a people. We subdue wild beasts and triumph over giants. No man or devil will dishonor me!" and she seized a torch, ready to fight with the devil she took Zan to be. She said some other words too, in a low singsong voice which could not quite be heard or understood—magic perhaps. Poor Zan was too sick to answer. He fell back on his bed, shivering and coughing, and when he sneezed she looked at him again with a new kind of wonder. This—boy—Dael's brother, was ill and needed help!

From then on, the girl redoubled her efforts to heal the invalid, rarely leaving his bedside. At night Zan had delirious dreams. The lion would come from nowhere to spring at him while Dael stood by, laughing cynically. It was not the cheerful laugh that Zan remembered, and it horrified him more than the lion's long fangs. As Zan slowly recovered his strength, and the evil nightmares left him, he questioned his caretaker. Her name was Lissa-Na, a priestess of a secret society dedicated to healing the sick and assisting women in childbirth. Na meant Healer. She told him that the cave in which he lay was holy, and forbidden to men. Blushing to his waist, Zan demanded of her why she had brought him to a place of women. She replied that it was permitted to bring the dying there for the final care that would usher them easily into the world of spirits. But that came out on the fourth day of Zan's recovery. He had hardly been able to speak when he asked the question most important to him: "Who knows that I am here?"

Some of the women and her servant knew. They had been gathering salt for the preservation of meat (which was one of their duties) when they had found him. Because he looked like Dael, they had assumed that Dael had fled his captivity and had gotten lost in the desert. At first they had thought he was dead (Lissa-Na sobbed a little when she said it), but looking closely, she had detected a little life stirring. Fearing he would be punished or even tortured for attempting escape (and here she suppressed another sob), she had brought him to this place of safety. No one would enter here but the Na women, who kept apart from the place where Dael was imprisoned. So it was unlikely that they would realize there were "two" Daels.

Zan was overjoyed, as Lissa-Na could readily see, to learn that his twin brother was still alive. "How is Dael?" he asked, and here again Lissa-Na was shaken with emotion. "He has been in that cage for over a year," she said. "He was given to the women of Na for a time, but he refused to do the work of women and was beaten." Zan winced painfully on his gentle brother's account. Lissa-Na lowered her eyes. "Now, I do not know what they make him do. They use him as they please, and throw scraps to him like a dog." She wiped away some tears with her fist.

"Can I see him?" Zan asked.

She told him that it would be difficult. The men of Noi would want to kill them both if they saw the brothers together, as they did their own twins at birth. "How can two people share one spirit?" she asked. Her eyes expressed a lingering doubt and fear.

Zan saw that Lissa-Na cared for Dael. For a moment the discovery caused him a sharp pang which he was unable to explain to himself. But he longed to see his brother, and was ready to rise from his sickbed to rescue him. "Lissa-Na, can you bring me a spear or at least a knife? I will need a weapon to get Dael away from his captors," and he checked to see that the sling was still tied around his waist.

Lissa knew better than to assist Zan in a reckless enterprise. She reminded him that there was nowhere to flee but into the desert where they would die if they were not well equipped for the journey. Zan was in no condition to travel, and neither was Dael. However, she promised to help them—at much risk to herself, as Zan knew—and her eyes lighted up at the prospect of delivering Dael from his suffering. She would find a way to bring him to the sacred cave.

"You care for my brother. Why? He is not one of yours."

"I do not deny it. When he first came here, sold to us by the wasp people, he was beautiful and gentle. You are quite different from him, although you look exactly alike. He was used so roughly that it made me weep, and later, when he was often in my presence, or where I could see his wretchedness, I came to love and pity him. I have never told anyone, but I gave him food—and kind words when I could. They keep him in a cage so small that he cannot fully stand up or lie down. I have longed to bring him here, but I dared not. The Na women would not have allowed it before, but now they think it proper."

Zan mused on what she had said. "If you can secretly bring him here, you can put him in my place. Then I could hide somewhere until we make our escape together."

Lissa-Na, who was by disposition soft-spoken and reserved, brightened with enthusiasm and swore she would attempt it. The prospect of seeing Dael filled each of them with a private happiness. But there was something in Lissa's words that stung Zan. "She 'loves and pities' Dael. She will 'put him in my place!'" he thought ruefully. Still his gratitude overwhelmed his jealousy and he eagerly awaited the night (for night it had to be) when the liberation could be brought to pass.

It was nine nights before it happened. Zan pretended extreme illness when members of her healing order were present, and Lissa-Na made ready a place of hiding. When she could, she brought food, articles for storing water, and tools, hiding them for the time of escape. She also obtained two spears, one at a time. All of these efforts were exceedingly dangerous, for violations of the laws of her people and the Na women were punishable by death. However, Lissa-Na enjoyed a certain respect among the Noi, and was not closely watched.

Finally one midnight as Zan lay alone in his supposed sickbed he saw by the faint light of the small fire a pair of legs coming through a hole in the roof of the cave— and then a second pair, descending down a long rope. (Zan had never seen twisted rope before, and examined it well when he had a chance.) The opening served the purpose of admitting light during the day, and was an exit for smoke. The legs belonged to Dael and Lissa-Na, who climbed down toward the fire, avoiding it when they got to the floor of the cave. Lissa was breathless and gaily laughing. Dael was silent. "Dael! Dael!" Zan cried, leaping from his bed.

When Dael heard his name he seemed not to know it, giving Zan a puzzled look, as if he did not know him either. Zan flew to Dael, embracing him with all of his strength. He was so glad to see Dael that he could have died of joy. But Dael, strangely quiet and surly, hardly returned his embrace. He just stood there like the imbecile column of stone that Zan had lately mistaken for his brother. Zan looked at him fully in the face. Dael was taller, with some hairs on his chin. Zan felt his own chin and it was the same. There was something else—a jagged furrow ascending Dael's brow that looked like the scar of a recent wound. Zan hugged him again and kissed his neck, unwilling to let him go. "Dael, I have come to rescue you." Dael did not respond. Zan looked at his scarred face with wonder and saw a blank. The happiness and play that had always been there before was gone. This laughing child looked as if he would never laugh again. For a moment Zan actually doubted that the youth in front of him was Dael. He scrutinized him as one would stare at a lost dog that might or might not be his. It was Dael, but how changed! The twinkle of his eyes was replaced by a leaden dullness, and his ever-present smile seemed to have died forever on his lips. Dael said nothing, and hardly even looked at Zan, but there was something in his lusterless eyes and expressionless face that was dangerous, startling, and deadly.

Lissa-Na put him in Zan's bed and prepared to hide Zan in a dark, unused alcove of the cave. Because it was night, and no one else was there, Zan could keep out of hiding for a while to talk with his brother. It had been a long time and he had much to tell. But Dael showed no interest in his brother's conversation, although he seemed to be listening. Zan wasn't even sure of that, but continued to speak excitedly of their family and of his confrontation with the lion, acquainting him with his name of honor, Zan-Gah. He showed Dael his scars, stealing a glance at Lissa-Na to see her reaction. Then he told him of his meeting with Aniah and of his adventures along the way. Dael said almost nothing, as if he were absorbed by some painful or perplexing memory. Zan could only guess what had happened to his gentle twin to work such a transformation in him, and he began to speak more softly, as one afraid to disturb a sick person.

Dael was soon missed. Warriors of Noi spent the next day searching for him, and eventually one was dispatched to inquire of him at the cave. Ab-Lunt presumed to enter, although he knew better than to go very far into its forbidden depths. He was an arrogant man, muscular and very hairy. He had a heavy club over his shoulder, made from the thighbone of a large animal. Presenting himself to Lissa-Na, who was the only female there, he told his errand, demanding to know who was lying within. Lissa tried to block the advance of this large, aggressive man, but she was no match for him. Dael rose from his bed, ready to submit himself to his captors, and perhaps hoping to spare Lissa any trouble. That was when Zan came out of his place of hiding and stood beside Dael, holding a spear.

Poor, stupid Ab-Lunt was frozen with fear. He gazed on the twins with horror as if confronted by twin devils. Dael walked up to Ab-Lunt, who did not move a muscle but stared straight across at Zan with wide-eyed paralysis, his face twisted into a grotesque, hairy mask. With no resistance whatever from the rigid, staring warrior, Dael took the coarse thighbone club from his grip. *Then it happened!* With the unnatural shriek of a wild animal Dael struck Ab-Lunt on the head with his own club. The blow was so violent that the man fell to the ground with a groan, his head split open and his brains bursting from his skull. He was dead. Yet that was not all. Dael kept beating him with mindless fury as if he did not know what he was doing. "Enough, Dael, enough!" Zan said, grabbing his wrist to prevent yet another blow. Dael looked up at his twin with a dazed, vacant stare, as though he had been awakened from a frightful dream, and listlessly dropped the weapon. What had once been Ab-Lunt lay on the ground, his shaggy head crushed to jelly and his blood forming a sticky pool.

Zan was sick at heart, and Lissa-Na was weeping and tearing her red hair. It was true that Dael had slain the man who would have imprisoned him, but the deed was so sudden and the manner of it so unspeakably brutal that Zan and Lissa-Na were shocked to the bottom of their souls. Lissa-Na could see that her life with the Noi people was over. Out of love for Dael she had betrayed all trust, and now his furious hand had brought down a man of Noi. The Na women might enter at any time, and raise an alarm, so there was nothing to do but hurry away. The body of Ab-Lunt had to be hidden in order to delay pursuit if only for a little while. They took the all-important store of food, water and other hidden supplies and made ready, dragging the horrible corpse to the same place of concealment. Dael did not help, but stood in the same spot, breathless and almost as stupefied as Ab-Lunt had been, so that Zan and Lissa had to drag him off too. It was plain to see that the landscape of Dael's soul was charred; the wind had blown a fire through and everything living had been burnt to blackness. The knowledge that the Noi would take vengeance upon him for the murder of Ab-Lunt seemed not to concern him. He had shut off the part of himself that feels pleasure, pain, or fear. But coming to himself, he followed Lissa, more than Zan. His face was firmly set, with his teeth tightened and one eyebrow of his deeply scarred forehead frowning. They whispered as they went. He said nothing.

The cave had appeared to be fairly limited in size, but as they turned around the curved wall a narrow opening was revealed. Lissa-Na led the way. By the light of their torches Zan beheld a place of wonder. "This is the womb of the earth—our most sacred place. We should not be here," Lissa said. "And I wish I had not been the one to defile it," she added to herself. The sanctuary was long and narrow, like a human intestine. On the walls and roof of the passage game animals had been vividly painted by the priestesses in black, red, and ochre. All of the beasts were depicted in actual size, and all faced in the same direction. "We must follow the way of the animals," said Lissa-Na, "and exit where they do."

After they had advanced into the depths of the cave for some time, Lissa-Na caused them to stop and to listen carefully for any noise of pursuit. They heard nothing but the dripping of water. With any luck the body of Ab-Lunt and their absence would not be discovered for some time.

Whether for fun or out of desperate anxiety, Dael suddenly let out a shrill and startling cry, shattering the silence and causing his companions to gasp with amazement as the echo screamed back again. Dael seemed not to be in mental contact with their situation. He laughed nervously, almost giggled, as if he had become a child again. Lissa hushed him and gently stroked his cheek and brow, and they went on.

The cave was very wet, which surprised Zan, for above ground all had been parched desert. Evidently there was fresh water in abundance, but he had not been lucky enough to have found it. They even came to an underground river fed by a concealed spring as they went deeper and lower into the cavern. The water seemed perfectly still, but when Zan stuck his spear in to determine its depth, the invisible current nearly took the weapon out of his hand. Where it was shallow he could see a few pale fish and eyeless salamanders. The further they went, the more the water dripped, sculpting the interior into fantastic shapes that glowed eerily in the light of their torches. Pointed shafts of stone descended from the ceiling or rose from the floor. Some, thin as reeds, barred off large sections of the cave and cast mysterious shadows. As they progressed, the stone took on ever more fabulous configurations. Rocky substance hung in folds like the living flesh of great fungi, or seemed to spout into geysers. The hardened stone tumbled and flowed as if it once had been soft and spongy stuff bubbling from the ground. Who would have known that the hollows of the earth held such mysteries! Then the color of these cursive forms changed abruptly from yellow to red, as if flowing with blood, and soon changed back again when the three went on.

The passage gradually narrowed so that advancing became difficult, but all at once the space opened dramatically to a great overhanging dome eaten hollow by the ages. Painted animals reappeared on the walls, seeming to stampede forward toward another narrow place. From the incessant dripping Zan guessed that they were under a river—the water supply of the Noi. The air was heavy with moisture and they could see each other's breath. Their torches sputtered, throwing forth a sulfurous light and immense, surging shadows.

At last they began going upward again, walking, climbing, and struggling. They spoke but little, but when they did their voices made ghostly, whispering echoes. In the silent darkness Dael screamed forth a reasonless yelp as sudden and startling as before, and hundreds of shrill-voiced bats were roused. "We are nearing the mouth of the cave. That is where the bats live," Lissa said, and with remarkable tenderness she again soothed Dael's agitation.

Far off they saw a glimmer of daylight reflecting off the dripping walls.

11 DAEL

As the three fugitives approached the opening, they felt with increasing force the lively wind that had pursued them from one end of the cave to the other. Its low-pitched, whistling moan was more noticeable now as they ascended the last few feet of the tunnel. Lissa-Na was the first to emerge into the brilliant light of day. From behind Zan saw the bright sunlight strike her blowing orange hair, turning it for a moment into fire. He could not help himself. He was on fire too—he loved her! But he said nothing—for what was there to say? The constant attentions she lavished on his brainsick brother told him where her affections lay. And if anything in the world could nurse his twin brother to restored health, it was the open and affectionate heart of Lissa-Na.

They did not know if they had been followed, either within the cave or over their heads. It was quite possible that a war party would be waiting for them nearby. Lissa, who was familiar with the area, scouted the terrain for pursuers lest they be ambushed. No one was there. When Zan finally regained his sense of direction he was able to inform Lissa of the path toward his home. Having neither desire nor choice but to go along, she led them to a shallow river which flowed in the direction Zan had pointed out. Zan, who had suffered so much from thirst and the desert's heat, was amazed to see a river along which he might have traveled had he known about it. He simply had not located it before or during the agonizing trek that had almost killed him. It was the lake of salt that had gotten his notice from a distance, and had unfortunately become the focus of his journey. Zan could not think of that lake without nausea. But now they could travel along a stream of fresh water. It seemed too good to be true!

Maybe it was! They had not gone very far when they realized that they were being followed closely by a band of several Noi warriors. There was absolutely no place to hide, nor did it seem likely that they could outrun these men; but they got ready to try. That in itself was dangerous. The blazing desert sun could be fatal to runners, and if they were forced to abandon the stream they would soon run out of anything to drink. True, Lissa-Na had always lived in this arid place, and knew any number of ways to stay alive. Survival was a game that Zan also knew how to play, but what chance had they against armed warriors in possession of an ample supply of water?

"Always face your enemy." These words of his father came back to him now. If he must be killed, let it be from the front, courageously, not from behind with the final wound in his back. But it was Lissa-Na who first turned to face the advancing men. "I am still a priestess of Na," she said proudly. "I do not run from churlish men of war! Turn and face them, and see what I will do."

Wondering at her courage and presence of mind, both brothers did as she bid them. She ordered them each to take one of her arms, to hold their spears straight out, and to move their legs as she did. She raised first one knee and then the other in a rhythmic, angular dance. "Do what I do," she yelled. Zan did as he was told, and Dael, who stood in awe of Lissa-Na, did his best to follow. Thus the three directly faced their enemies arm-in-arm, performing a slow and stately measure, while the twins simultaneously brandished their spears. Lissa-Na began to sing loudly an eerie, high-pitched chant, and continued to lead them in rhythmic movement. "Sing!" she commanded, and the brothers joined in her chant: *Oa-ee-YU! Oa-ee-YU.* The sun at their backs made a luminous halo of their hair.

Suddenly Zan understood. The three were physically representing an ominous mystic symbol. It was the same protective emblem he had seen carved into the slab of stone when he had first entered this desert land. Its purpose had been *to frighten people away.* Would it work now? The emblem's magical power would be recognized by the Noi warriors, but could they possibly be warded off by a mere dance?

The result of this maneuver was wonderful. Ten Noi men stopped in their tracks, looked on for a moment in amazement at the radiant trio, and ran away in utter panic. What had frightened them so? "Keep moving exactly as I do," Lissa said. "Do not stop until they are gone!" They both continued to follow her lead, but with a difference in the way they felt. Zan was greatly relieved to see that he was not going to die; Dael seemed completely indifferent, and only mechanically did Lissa's bidding.

Zan was puzzled. Why would ten grown men flee from three youngsters? Only later did he realize what had happened. True, the symbol they had acted out held a fearful potency among the Noi, but that alone would not have been sufficient to repulse them. Was it that the three had faced them and shown no fear? Perhaps. But what had been most frightening to the men of Noi was the sight of *twins*—for they had been completely unaware of Zan's existence. None but dead Ab-Lunt had seen them together, and the sight had turned him to stone! Now, a woman of magic, as Lissa-Na was respected to be, was flanked by a devil who had divided himself and his spirit into *two parts!* And why not next into four? The men of Noi would long afterwards talk with superstitious dread about the "demon" who had lived unrecognized in their presence.

And so they escaped the vengeance of the Noi, although Lissa-Na continued to fear their return once they had consulted with the priestesses. The three sped on for a long time before they could safely stop and camp. Another cold night passed (the desert can be surprisingly cold once the sun has gone down) before they dared to build a fire. With three it was easier to make fires, build shelters, and even bring down game. Dael showed little interest in Zan's sling, but Lissa-Na was fascinated with it. Before long she had fashioned one for herself, and with practice became adept at its use. It proved its value when they were surrounded by a pack of hungry wolves. That happened on the fourth day of their retreat. Zan could not have fought them off alone, but he and Lissa together pelted them with stones fired with such force and accuracy that they withdrew whimpering—except for the one that Dael had gored with his spear.

Lissa's knowledge of the desert, where she had always lived, enabled the wanderers to stay alive and well. There were all sorts of edibles and liquid sources that Zan had not dreamed of when he had been there alone, and they were able to stay with the river stream. Ages of flow had worn such a deep channel in the desert soil that they found themselves below the surface of the land, which itself provided some shelter. The three were covered with dust and sand when a rare desert rain came. The twins raised their mouths to the downpour as they had when they were little boys, while the river swelled and foamed with renewed energy. The next day the entire desert was gorgeous with bloom. Even Dael seemed to notice. Lissa busied herself with gathering honey-flavored edibles, and Dael was pleased when he tasted them.

That night, when they had settled in a sheltered place in the river's deep rut and had built a fire there, Zan decided to try to talk to Dael. During the journey his twin had said almost nothing, but had seemed intensely involved with his own bitter thoughts. As they sat apart Zan would glance at Dael, still almost doubting that it was the same person he had once played games with. Dael's face was glowing in the light of the flame, but it was rigid except that his forehead sometimes furrowed or twitched, as if his spirit were deeply engaged in an invisible battle. Zan could not guess what poisonous scorpion had bitten, had infected his gentle spirit. Pleasant weather did not make him cheerful nor bad weather sad. He seemed not to feel the intermittent breeze nor to delight in anything, but was as one set alone in a dark place from which there was no exit. Yes, it was Dael, but....

When Zan approached his brother, Dael was startled and his lips visibly tightened. He did not want to talk. "Soon we will be home," Zan began with some hesitation. "What fun it will be to fish in Nobla as we used to do." He recalled how much Dael once wanted to find the source of their river, but a sidelong glance at his brother now convinced him that Dael no longer wished to go fishing, and cared not where the river came from.

"Dael, what happened in the land of the Noi? Would it not be better to tell me?" Zan waited for an answer but he did not get one. Some minutes later, when Zan no longer expected a reply, Dael's lips began to tremble and he muttered something. Zan did not have to ask him to repeat his words, for Dael kept on muttering the same thing over and over: "The night came and they took me.... The night came and they took me.... "

"Dael, all that is past. We are free! We will be home soon, and imagine what rejoicing will receive us! Wumna, our mother, thinks that you are dead!"

"I am, Zan, to her and to you."

Lissa-Na, who had been listening from a distance, came up to Dael and held his shoulders with loving hands. "No, Dael," she said softly. "You will be like this dry desert, which receives a little rain and surprises us all with its new flowers." Dael stared intently at the fire and said nothing.

In the morning Dael lay down to drink from the stream and Zan lay down beside him. Seeing their remarkably similar reflections side by side, Dael moved away. "We are just alike, Dael," Zan could not help saying.

"No, Zan, we are not alike. I do not wish to have a twin."

"Why not, Dael? We were born on the same day."

"I cannot tell you why! I can never tell anyone!" And nothing Zan could say or do would entice Dael to say another word. But that night Dael announced that he would not be going home.

"Not home? What will you do?" Zan asked incredulously. "How can you hope to live in this deadly place?" Dael did not answer right away, but Zan understood that he had made up his mind.

"I will find a cave just as you did."

Zan did not try to dissuade his brother. He knew that Dael had suffered so much for two years that the damage to his spirit could not be undone all at once.

Zan-Gah, who had killed a lion, could not slay a beast he could not see—a monster that was consuming his twin. He withdrew and left him to Lissa's care. The persistent, vivid memory of Ab-Lunt's horrible death wore sorely on his mind, and doubtless on theirs as well.

The next day Zan changed his tactics. Instead of approaching Dael, he spoke continually to Lissa-Na about his family, which he described in loving terms as they walked along. This was for Dael's benefit, however, who was intended to hear most of what he said. He told her about the lion hunt and the name of honor Aniah had given him, and of his later visit to the great elder. He told her about his uncle, Chul, on whom he lavished much praise. Then he touched on beauty and respect, but mostly he spoke of the deep bond he shared with his family.

Suddenly Dael, who had maintained a complete and stubborn silence, angrily spat at his feet. His face was torn between rage and pain. "I am no longer good like you, Zan-Gah (he emphasized "Gah"), and I am no longer your twin. I do not want your company, and I can never go home. I wish you would kill me with your spear and leave my body to be eaten by animals. Or show me that gorge you mentioned that I might throw myself into it and rot at its bottom, unseen by anyone!"

Oddly, after that outburst, consisting of more words than he had spoken for many days, Dael's ghost seemed quieted. Lissa-Na did not cease to speak to him and soothe him as best she could. She would hold his cheek to hers, whispering and singing softly, assuaging his mental hurt that he might forget, at least for moments, whatever it was that molested and tormented him. This much success she had: Dael did not repeat his wish to go away.

The river they were following passed between two great hills and suddenly came to an end, plunging over a high cliff to a lake many feet below. It was a moment before Zan recognized the place that had once impressed him with its exceeding beauty. But they had to be watchful, for they had arrived at the lands of the wasp people. From his high perch Zan surveyed the entire area. He could see several clusters of their nest-like dwellings in the trees, noting that they were distant enough from one another that the three might be able to pass unnoticed between them. Night was at least two hours away. Perhaps they could cross the area of danger before it became too dark to see, while still enjoying the advantage of twilight, which was that they would not be so highly visible.

There was a roundabout path that descended from the top of the cliff on one side, leading around the lake and directly between two of the wasp clans. It was nearly dark when they reached the place which they hoped to slip through. It was a small area forested with a few ancient pines, and carpeted with a bed of soft needles that would cushion their steps. As they passed, they could see the camp fires of the two clans, and could even hear their voices overhead. Their absolute quiet would be necessary if the passage was to succeed, and neither Zan nor Lissa dared to breathe the least whisper as they tiptoed carefully over the carpet of needles. Above their heads the wind brushed the tops of the trees, exhaling a

hissing noise that obscured the rustle of their feet. But
all of their fearful precautions were wasted when Dael,
possibly troubled by the silence, began to scream and
whoop like a madman careless of his life. Nothing Lissa
and Zan could do would calm him down, and they were
soon surrounded by a band of armed wasp men. At its
head was the blond-bearded Naz! What evil luck to fall
into their hands, and especially his, after having barely
escaped the Noi warriors!

Naz and his spearmen had no fear of twins as the Noi
people did. When after a moment they recognized Zan,
they only were surprised to discover that their numbskull
servant of old had a double. As for the third, the flame-
haired Lissa-Na, Naz immediately claimed her for his
own—above the objections of several of the men—and
grabbed her by the wrist. That was a fatal mistake. In his
long life, Zan never could forget what followed. Dael, his
head bowed but still holding his spear, let loose a terrible,
paralyzing scream and stabbed Naz in the throat. Naz's
proud thoughts had been far from death, but now, with
his eyes still open, he fell to the ground a corpse. The
other men were much astonished, and seizing all three
they pricked them with their venomous spears and let
them fall down in helpless agony. When they recovered
hours later they were in a cage that was strong enough
to hold a bear.

That night they were sufficiently miserable. Zan now
had no reason to pretend that he was stupid, and judging
from the way he was addressed, he gathered that he would
fool no one with the old subterfuge. Speaking to the
guards directly in their own language, he asked through

the bars of the cage what their fate would be. He received only a coarse guffaw for an answer. Then one of them asked where he had come from. Fearing that they might all be sent back to the Noi in pieces, he told them that they grew up in the land beyond the great chasm in the earth, which they had expected to cross before they had been taken prisoner. The men laughed again. "You will see it but you will never cross it. You will visit its bottom! You have killed, and now you must die the Terrible Death, which we reserve for special enemies. Then we will cross it ourselves at the secret place, right over your shattered skulls, and take revenge on your coward people, for we know them well!"

It was about three hours before dawn. Zan and Lissa were still wide awake, although Dael, heedless of death, had fallen into a deep sleep. So had their guards. In this captivity Zan visualized the horrible death that was planned for them, but he also thought of Naz. He had never detested any human being as much. But was Naz—proud, stubborn, and with a certain blindness—so very different from Zan? Then he contemplated Dael, sleeping like an exhausted child. He was not sorry that Naz was dead; only that Dael had killed him. He nearly wept to think that his happy, smiling twin had twice shed blood without the least remorse. This gentle brother, whom he had always tried to protect, had become so violent, so dangerous, that Zan was almost afraid to be near him. With these troubling thoughts Zan looked gloomily out of his cage into the dark and silent night. Behind the strong trees that supported the wasp-dwellings was a full moon, but Zan could not see it. What he did see was a bush—that started to move! It appeared to be a large animal in the blackness coming between the trees. Was it a bear? It was too dark to tell. For a long time the animal stopped moving, possibly wondering whether it dared to come any closer to the camp. Zan envied its freedom. If only that bear were in this cage and he and his companions were able to roam or find shelter in the woods!

Slowly and very cautiously, the creature came forward a little; and suddenly it reared up on its hind legs like a huge, imposing ape. Yet Zan saw dimly at last that it was neither a bear nor an ape. Emerging from the opaque darkness was a gigantic man! It was Chul! Zan was never so glad to see anyone in his life! He roused Dael even as Chul dispatched each of the guards with a single blow of his great fist. Then grabbing two of the bars of their pen, Chul snapped them like twigs and Zan and Lissa stepped out, ready to flee for their lives. "Come Dael, come," Zan whispered urgently, but Dael *would not come!* "No, Zan," he said. "I do not wish to go home. I will not."

It was said that Chul was slow-witted, and it was true. But more than most, he had powerful and sure instincts. He saw at once that Dael was not himself—was sick—that something awful must have happened to work an earthquake in his mind. Chul did not pause to argue. Grabbing Dael by his arm, he flung him across his mighty shoulders and ran so fast that Zan and Lissa could scarcely keep up with him and his load. Dael was too dispirited to resist.

In his simplicity, Chul had never doubted that he would find both Zan-Gah and Dael. He had made careful preparations, bringing large supplies of food and water and leaving caches of both in caves, tree hollows, and under rocks all along the way. There were a couple of weapons too. They soon retrieved some necessities, especially the spears. The dawn was breaking and they were going on a downhill slope toward the land of red rocks where there would be many hiding places. Meanwhile they had to make haste. Their footprints were easily visible in the dusty ground, and it might not be long before spearmen were on their trail. Because they were traveling downhill, the wasp men, from their higher vantage point, would be able to see their progress from a considerable distance. They could not stop to eat or make a fire, at least until they had crossed the great gorge that was supposed to be Zan's burial place.

In telling his guards the night before where they were hoping to go, Zan had not been wise. The wasp men knew exactly in which direction to pursue them, and might well have caught them quickly if they had not delayed. But they had been preparing for a larger attack against the five clans, their old enemies. Thus, Zan's small band had a whole day to flee before they were followed—not by one but by seven clans of barbaric, fantastically painted warriors. It was almost an army.

When Zan's group entered the land of red rocks they had to stop and camp whether they wanted to or not. They had hardly slept in days, nor eaten more than their bare subsistence required. Zan and Chul were accustomed to deprivation, but Dael was weakened by whole years of captivity. Lissa-Na, unused to either long travel or lack of comfort, was visibly in danger of collapse. In time, as they walked between the high, protective walls of the red cliffs, Zan recognized his former dugout shelter by the great death's-head configurations. Curiously, none of the party but he saw skull forms in the rocks, and Zan did not point them out. Showing them the easiest way to ascend to the dugout, he received an unlikely surprise when he found that it was already occupied! A young lad showed himself and called out to Zan-Gah in a familiar voice. It was Rydl!

Warm (if astonished) greetings and introductions followed. Zan explained to his companions how Rydl had befriended him in his time of trouble, and he was well received. Rydl finally understood what a twin was, and gazed long and curiously at both of them, giving a frightened glance at Chul as well. Rydl explained that his aid to Zan a few weeks earlier had been quickly suspected by the wasp men, and feeling sure that his kinsmen would force the truth out of him, he ran away, hiding in the red dugout and enjoying life there for the most part. He showed Zan the sling he had made for himself, and demonstrated how adept he had become with it. This surprised Zan as he remembered how little Rydl formerly had been interested in his invention. Trying it out, Chul responded to the weapon as Rydl had when he was younger—with awkwardness and little profit. It kept getting tangled, and Chul tended to hit himself with his own rock. None guessed at the time how important the invention of the sling would be to the future of Zan's people.

There was no time for this "plaything." The exhausted party had to sleep for a few hours and quickly get on their way. Rydl, learning who might be pursuing them, decided to go along lest he be seized by his people and flung into the bottomless chasm. He too slept in preparation for a journey. Chul was the first to awake, roused by a distant noise. He immediately woke the others and bade them listen. The sound they heard was like remote thunder, and Zan took it to be an approaching storm; but Chul, allowing his jaw to drop as he listened intently, declared that it was the beat of drums. The wasp men were coming!

Chul instructed them to gather their things quickly. It sounded like an army and it was getting closer. As in a hunt the wasp warriors were announcing their advance with a dreadful clamor in the hope of driving their quarry to the edge of the abyss. Zan thought of the lion hunt when a similar method had been used. "Why should we allow them to drive us into their trap?" Zan asked. "We could wait here and try to slip behind their lines. I am not afraid of their noises!" Even as he spoke the drumbeats grew louder, now accompanied by a savage, deep-voiced chant of war: *Ah ah UH! Ah ah UH! Ah ah UH!*

"To be trapped in this hole like frightened animals?" Chul responded. "No! We know where the crossing is, and we can beat them to it! If they get there first, our people will have no warning of the attack. And they will place guards at the bridge to take us when we try to cross." There was no time for debate. They were roughly jolted into action by the regimented, inexorable reverberation of the drums. Chul led and the others followed him—except for

Dael, who followed Lissa-Na. And still the coarse chant and thunderous beat pursued them, ever louder.

The wasp men progressed at a steady, deliberate pace, eventually pausing to camp for the night. They were in no great hurry, satisfied that nothing could stop their advance. Zan's party made no such pauses, but sped toward the great cleft with its single crossing; so they were actually able to increase the distance that separated them from the drums and arrive at the chasm well before them. Unfortunately, they could not at once find the dead tree which served as the only bridge, and by the time they did, the wasp men were in sight, beating a note of terror, and grumbling their dull cry of battle. Rydl went first, dancing across with practiced step like a cat. Lissa-Na, whom Zan had come to respect as a very courageous person, crossed next with no sign of fear, her red hair flying. Dael followed, and then Zan. In the middle of the crossing Dael suddenly stopped and looked down into the stupefying depths of the chasm. Perhaps he was asking himself whether or not to end his life then and there. Guessing at his thought, Lissa called to him and extended her hand. He looked at her face for four or five seconds, looked down again, and then—took her hand and went across. Zan was close behind.

The wasp men with their eerily painted faces and red-tipped spears were close, and the tumult of their drums beat like astounding thunder. It was Chul's turn to cross, *but he did not take it!* Instead he grasped in his huge hands the end of the gnarled old log that served as a bridge. It was the small end, the top of what had once been a tree, and with a titanic effort wrenched the trunk from its seat on the other side and sent it toppling and crashing by starts to the bottom of the abyss. To save his friends Chul was sacrificing himself! There was no crossing now, and the spearmen were rushing toward him. An agile dodge and the stroke of his club sent the foremost of them to his death. Meanwhile Zan, Lissa-Na, and Rydl were using their slings to good effect, giving Chul some relief. But it could not be long before he would be cut down by the multitudes that were approaching. It was Rydl who saved him. Calling loudly to him, he signaled a spot nearby that was a little narrower than the fissure generally was. Nowhere was the split in the earth very wide, but this spot alone might possibly be crossed by a very large, athletic, and daring man. Taking a desperate run, Chul leapt across to a colossal boulder on the other side, grabbing it with his very fingernails and holding onto it for his life. To his dismay, he heard a grating sound that sickened him. Under the violent shock of his weight the boulder had begun to move! With a final dauntless effort, even as spears were being hurled at him, Chul reached the top of the great rock, which slowly was collapsing under him. At the last crucial moment he was able to jump onto the far side and evade the assault, while the immense stone, like the gnarled log before, tumbled and crashed for a full minute to the bottom of the chasm.

12 THE COUNCIL OF ELDERS

The drums stopped. The wasp men, gathering at the edge of the cliff, first gazed into its awesome depths and then outward at the escaping fugitives. Once at a safe distance, Zan and his group did not look back. Several of the warriors threw their spears in sheer rage, although they knew that their targets were well out of range. Then they turned their wrath on their leader, as though it had been his fault that their intended victims had gotten away. Before long they were all arguing among themselves. They were indeed a quarrelsome people, swift to anger and far from unified—except in their shared desire for pillage.

Not one of their large group dared attempt the leap that Chul had made, and the next point of passage over this great schism in the earth was three days away. A few were ready to make the trek, but the greater number were not. Unnerved by the physical power of Chul and the inept beginning they had made, they decided to go home for a while to regroup their forces and salve their morale. Later they would build another bridge, when they had the materials they needed at hand. This was finally agreed upon, but not without such violent dissension that they came near to attacking each other.

It need hardly be said with what surprise, joy, and excitement the return of Zan-Gah, Dael and Chul was received. From a distance, Thal recognized the two familiar globes of hair as in former days. How happy he was to see his two sons together whom he never thought to see again! When they arrived, Wumna, not believing her eyes and afraid the vision would disappear, nearly fell down from sudden happiness; while the father stared in wonder at his boys, now taller and softly whiskered. Zan, slim and grown, thought that his mother had shrunk, and that Siraka-Finaka seemed even smaller than he remembered. Siraka-Finaka completely ignored Zan and Dael, considering only the giant before her. She pounded her husband's hairy chest with her little fists to make certain that he was real. Chul lifted her off her feet, embracing her and his children as he never had before. Then he twirled his war club over his head with a whoop of triumph joined in by one and all. Unnoticed at first, Lissa-Na and Rydl were accepted and welcomed as the friends of Zan-Gah, and Chul was not slow to tell how Rydl had saved him from sure destruction. Zan, too, informed his family that Lissa-Na had been his healer and friend. Wumna squinted her eyes and looked narrowly at her for a moment, and Siraka-Finaka examined her red hair in wonder, as at the plumage of an exotic bird. But Lissa was soon made to feel at home.

That night before the fire, conversation turned to serious matters. Thal was visibly older, and white hairs had appeared in his dark beard. He was more somber than Zan had ever seen him. The feud between the clans had begun again. It was the Hru who had broken the truce. They had gradually regained their strength once they had gotten some food. Zan remembered the rabbit he had given them when they were too hungry to hunt or attend to their own needs. Emboldened by Chul's absence, their defensiveness had changed to aggressive hostility, and although no one yet had been killed, some were seriously wounded.

"Friends," Zan said, "I must depart again to visit Aniah as I promised to do if I should return, and I must bring Dael with me if he will go. We cannot afford our hatred. I have reason to believe that the wasp men will be coming in great force, and we must stand together against them once again if we are to survive."

Very early the next day, Thal and Chul walked with the twins most of the way as their guards, but on approaching the dwelling of Aniah they remained behind. Their presence would only aggravate matters. If peace could be made, Zan-Gah alone could make it.

The word soon spread throughout the clans that Zan-Gah had returned with his brother. How this became known so quickly was a mystery, although not a difficult one; for although the men spoke only within their own clans, the women mixed secretly at times, sometimes for religious reasons. Generally, the women were less separated by hatred than their husbands. It was their own sufferings that they cared about, not the rancor and prejudices of their men.

When Zan and Dael approached the northern clan, they were welcomed in a more friendly fashion than ever. Zan-Gah, the hero of the lion hunt, was now also seen as the determined champion who had risked all to recover his brother and twin. Aniah clasped their hands, feasted them, and gave them audience. He looked at Dael with curiosity, for he could see that he was much changed. He observed that Dael said nothing, and stood behind Zan-Gah like his shadow. Zan had a great deal to tell, but he confined himself to the wasp people. He told Aniah how he had narrowly escaped, and how the might of Chul had temporarily prevented a massive invasion. "The wasp people are determined," he said, "to destroy us or make slaves of us," adding that many, perhaps two hundred had come at them.

Aniah had the look of one who is groaning inwardly with pain, his brow newly entrenched with a leader's woe. "It is hardly seven days since we were at each other's throats," he said. "Of all the five clans there is not one that does not feel aggrieved about something."

"Hear me, Aniah," Zan said with an intensity that surprised the old man. "We must unite. We have no choice! It is only by good fortune that the wasp men are not here this very day! I have struggled with land and weather, with enemies and fierce animals, as you have. But always the chief struggle was with myself! We must fight down our passions and our rages before we can defeat the greatest of our enemies." Then he added: "I know that you are a great man, older and wiser than I. But when did wisdom make war when it was not necessary, and neglect it when it was? Let us use our wisdom and your leadership to end this bloody strife."

Aniah was amazed at the manly change that had taken place in one whom he remembered as a boy. With his hand over his mouth, and furrowing his aged, wrinkled forehead, he thought deeply over what Zan-Gah had said. He stirred the fire with a stick and after a long pause declared firmly at last: "There is only one man who can pacify our clans and lead us to a truce."

"And who is that, Aniah?"

"*You*, Zan-Gah! *You* are the only man among us who has the admiration and love of all! When you slew the man-eating lion you won the hearts of everyone, and your return with your lost brother just as you promised has gained increased respect!"

Zan was gratified by this speech, not only for Aniah's praise, which he much valued, but because Aniah had called him a *man*. Was he a man now and no longer a boy?

"The Hru will not receive me," Aniah continued. "The Luta will not welcome your father or your uncle. There is no one but you!"

"Then hear my plan, Aniah, for I will need your help."

Zan's project was first to hold a council to which each of the five clans would send two elders and one woman of their selection. The meeting place was to be the exact spot where together they had killed the lion. It was chosen deliberately to remind those present of their former unity and how well it had served them. Aniah saw no reason to include the women, but Zan insisted that his plan could not succeed without their participation. Zan personally visited all of the five tribes, and was well received by every one of them. Even the truculent Hru chieftains made an honored place for him at their fires. Since his return with Dael, Zan's prestige had soared, so that there was none save Aniah who was more highly respected among the peoples.

There was little resistance to the idea of a meeting once the elders of the clans became acquainted with the impending danger of an attack by the wasp men— although each and every one protested against the presence of females. Zan had a special reason for wishing to include them. Not least was his certain knowledge that the women hated the feud with all of their hearts, and not much less the masculine vanity that fed it. They would tip the scales in favor of Zan's project, and be a force for moderation among their men. "Bring no weapons," Zan told them, "but carry some wood there and bring food if you have any. I swear you will not be sorry."

When the tribesmen heard that Aniah favored the council, women included, and that he himself promised to be there, all sensed that they dared not stay behind while great actions were being concluded. So everybody went.

They met when the sun was high in the sky. (It was useless to expect men at war with each other to come weaponless at night, vulnerable to any treachery.) The men approached proudly, their women behind them. Character was deeply carved on every brow. They were mostly old warriors like Aniah, their hair whitened by age, and like him lean and muscular and covered with scars. From the Hru came Morda, the haggard chief who, long ago, had turned his back on Zan to kick dust in his direction. Morda had regained his strength and with it his haughty insolence. His shaggy brother stood beside him—a ragged branch of the same tree. One chief had a hideous gap where his eye once had been. He was the one that Thal said had been mauled by a lion. Another, his side teeth long since broken out by the blow of a club, exhibited a black hole in their place. Still another lacked a hand, which had been taken from him when he had been a prisoner—until Thal and Chul had succeeded in rescuing him from his tormentors. None of these battle-scarred men was handsome, but every one of them possessed the noble beauty residing in pride, honor, and manly dignity. The women, too, bore themselves with a statuesque dignity appropriate to their new role.

Zan-Gah appeared cloaked with the skin of the lion he had slain. Holding no spear, but only the staff that signified that he meant to speak, he stood before them like a stately pillar. He had grown taller since any there had seen him. Difficult trials had lent him both dignity and wisdom, and all waited eagerly to hear what he would say. None could look at Zan-Gah without detecting his deep sense of purpose and resolve. In the lion hunt, one man commented, Zan-Gah had stood behind his father, but now Thal and Chul were standing behind Zan-Gah. They also noticed that Siraka-Finaka had come. She and some other women were building a fire. Zan, anxious that they should not be perceived as servants only, assisted them.

The meeting began and all were silent when Zan-Gah started to speak. He stood in their presence like a tall, slender tree in front of a group of ancient, gnarled oaks. Long he remained there wondering how to begin. "Friends, brothers, and sisters," he finally said. "On this very spot we all united together for our good against a dangerous wild beast. Although I was fortunate enough to strike the fatal blow, and though I wear the animal's skin today, it was *our cooperation alone* that made that victory possible. We had differences then too, but we understood that it was necessary to work together to achieve our ends. It is necessary again!"

He told them of his captivity with the wasp people and how their army had pursued them to the great cleft in the earth. The listeners learned of the feats of Chul with wonder. Chul the giant blushed in spite of himself beneath his ragged beard, so that some smiled and all huffed out grunts of approval. Zan continued: "The wasp men will not give up. I know for a fact that they mean to kill us or carry us off. That is why I beg you to unite—to put aside your ancient quarrels and thoughts of honor in a foolish cause. For when was honor to be gained from stupidity—and is it not the worst stupidity to fight your friends and leave yourself naked to your enemies?"

Several chiefs growled or muttered their anger and defiance. One gaunt and sinewy elder with deep, glittering eyes prepared to speak. He was known to all as Kragg. Kragg's scars told his story, and he wore the stern demeanor of one who had maintained his integrity through a thousand hardships and conflicts. Zan yielded the staff to him. "It has always been thus, as long as I can remember," he said with his gravel voice. "My own brother was killed when we were young, and I have sworn revenge. He died when the moon was new, and with every new moon I renew my oath. I know some of you have made similar oaths. Can we with honor break them?"

Siraka-Finaka was not shy. Aflame with indignation she seized the stave from the old warrior and pounded the earth with it, demanding to be heard. It was the first time in the long history of the clans that a woman had spoken her mind in a council. "Hear me, elders," she cried above the clamor. "Which of you would lose a child or a brother—which woman here would lose a husband or son—because of stubborn pride or anger over something that happened so long ago that we cannot even remember what it was? I refuse henceforth to cook meat and to chew hides to feed and clothe fools!" The women, silent until now, murmured their approval of this speech. The men looked at each other, and their expressions were not happy ones.

Chul spoke next, and his words were few: "I am sorry, Aniah, that I slew your kinsman."

Taking up the staff, Aniah replied: "In our long war I have killed too—and when I did I myself died a little each time, even though many have praised me for my deeds. I would gladly bring back all of my enemies to recover one friend." A tear rolled down a wrinkled cheek that had never held one before. "We have been fools! Fools! Quick to anger and slow to wisdom!"

Something was happening so dramatic and unexpected that Zan was taken aback. These great, proud, life-bitten chiefs were saying that *they were sorry!* Zan could hardly believe his ears! Taking the staff again he said with a clear voice, "Let us seal a permanent peace with each other in order to stand firmly against our true enemies. Here is my proposal: Let this group of men *and women* be called the council of elders, and let it supervise all marriages. Henceforth, let no one take a wife from his own clan but with their special permission, rarely to be given. Rather, let us achieve a marriage of the clans by choosing from outside of our own, as we never yet have done. Swear to this and we become a single, unified people, and not five quarreling bands. Swear to this, and to abandon our ingrown hatreds, and we become a *nation* capable of standing up to the wasp men or any other invader."

The elders consented with loud grunts of approval. Making a ring about their fire and each taking the hand of the nearest person, they swore. Zan-Gah administered the oath. Then he announced that there was further business. "In return for this vow, and to show my confidence in our new unity, I am going to present you with a gift—two gifts."

Zan paused to catch his breath, a little bit afraid of what he was about to do.

13 THE LAST BATTLE

"I have two new powerful weapons," Zan declared, "to be used against our enemies, not each other—fatal to *them*, not to ourselves. The first is the red poison of the wasp men." This announcement caused a sensation among the elders, for they knew its power. Zan raised his voice above the hubbub: "I lived with them for a whole year and learned about their preparation, and now I can give you some of that poison to anoint your spears. Yours will be as deadly as theirs!" Zan did not tell them how it was made, however. Prudence told him to withhold that secret until the new peace had stood the test of time. He still feared that the poisoned spears might, in moments of rage, be directed against their own allies.

But he reluctantly decided to reveal the second secret. Zan now told them about the sling he had invented, because it was necessary for the clans to arm and prepare themselves against the wasp people without delay. Zan and Lissa-Na had made ten slings, and he distributed one to each of the men. An exhibition of its power saved him words. Placing in his own sling a piece of a chalky rock that he had selected especially for the purpose, Zan suddenly flung it against a large boulder. The result was dramatic. The soft rock hit so forcefully that it broke into powder and wafted away on the breeze. Zan showed them again, and the chalk became smoke again. The elders were wide-eyed! "You must make more of these slings for yourself. I will show your warriors how to use them, and they must practice until they are proficient. We must hurry! There is not very much time!"

Zan demonstrated the sling again several times, and most of the elders tried it, awkwardly at first but with gradually increasing success. As Zan showed the weapon he explained: "The sling has a number of advantages. A supply of stones is almost always available. You can bring lots of them with you, and if you use them up you can readily get more. That is not true of spears; and the rocks fly farther than one can throw a spear, so that you can keep a safe distance from the enemy and still attack him with deadly force. Also, they are light to carry and easy to conceal. I hid mine on my waist for a whole year and yet the wasp men did not know that I was armed!" This brought laughter and applause from Zan's audience.

For several days thereafter, Zan helped the fighting men to make slings and learn to use them. As had been his own case, it took considerable practice before any of them could handle the weapon effectively; but with diligent effort even clumsy Chul became very accurate. It was said that to be hit with a rock slung by this giant was either to die or to *wish* to die! The men set up targets and competed against each other as in a game. It was a revelation to them that their rivalry need not be destructive or fraught with hate. They became so remarkably skilled that together they were a formidable force.

Other methods of war were practiced too, notably the use of the envenomed spear. Poisoned, it was more dangerous to handle, as a couple of accidents proved to their sorrow. Chul was chosen to be their leader as they prepared themselves to go into battle. No one pressed Dael to fight, but a new ferocious liveliness showed his friends that nothing but death would keep him away. He longed to be revenged on those who first had taken him captive, and the thought of it lit his eyes with an unpleasant fire.

When the wasp men came, they did not come quietly. It was their practice to terrify their enemies before a major attack, rather than using surprise or stealth. From a distance sentinels heard them coming, well before they saw them. Drums of war and the savage chant of *Ah ah UH! Ah ah UH!* rumbled from afar. They had brought a light bridge, assembled at their dens, with which they had spanned the deep gulch. Now they appeared in great numbers, and it was a horrid sight. Seeming to wriggle toward them were the same human "centipedes" that Zan had observed while he was their prisoner. Each consisted of about thirty men marching in pairs with dance-like steps, deliberately winding as they went, and moving both arms and legs in unison to the rhythm of their chant: *Ah ah UH! Ah ah UH! Ah ah UH! Ah ah UH!* There were seven such groups—many-legged worms, ready to destroy anything in their path. Their total well outnumbered Zan's warriors. In preparing his clansmen, Zan had already described this method of attack. Except for the fear it caused, it actually was not a very good formation, he said. A rock or a spear thrown at one wasp warrior would hit the second man if it missed the first, so that few spears would be wasted or fail to bring someone down. Thus, despite the dire clamor of grunts and hisses, Zan's people were ready and undaunted.

When Chul signaled the attack it was launched abruptly, so that a fusillade of stones assailed these grotesque battle formations. Many wasp men fell before they were close enough to use their spears. Another barrage of stones completely broke and disorganized their ranks, and after a third, Zan's people rushed at them with their sharpened, red-tipped lances. Dael, among the foremost, fought with reckless bravery like a fiend, killing one after another in a feast of blood. He had no fear of death. Perhaps he still desired it. He thrust his spear into the belly of a wasp man whom he greeted by name, and ruthlessly pulled it out of his howling victim. Kicking the dying man in the face with all his might, he swung around to find another mark for his fury—and ran into his twin. Although Zan was his mirror image, Dael nearly killed him too before he realized who it was. Then, his face changing suddenly, he retired and let the others finish the battle.

A single formation of wasp warriors had held aloof, observing the battle from a higher position a short distance away. The others were in such a state of disarray that they were no longer a threat. With a wild yell Chul led the attack against this separate reserve of men. Fusillades of stones again broke the enemy ranks and poison-tipped spears incapacitated many as they fled. Helpless with pain, these unlucky wretches were seized and without mercy flung screaming into the ghastly depths of the abyss they had so foolishly crossed. No prisoners were taken.

The rest of the wasp men were beaten, fleeing in terror and moreover deeply dismayed to find that the secret of their poison had been discovered. The clans would no longer be troubled by them. Within two years they had all perished, weakened by defeat and by their constant dissension and blood-feuds. Indeed, three of their principal leaders were murdered in their sleep by ambitious rivals, and the internal wars that followed were terrible. When a deadly plague struck—not for the first time—the wasp people were wiped from the face of the earth. Only Rydl survived, newly adopted and befriended by Zan's people.

———————————————

For the second time in his life Zan-Gah was lifted as a hero onto the shoulders of his companions. (No one attempted to lift the well-deserving Chul!) Three days of wild celebration followed, held mainly by the great rock, Gah, from which Zan had gotten his name. These were men whose virtues were of the crudest sort. Many were the arts they had not yet mastered; but they knew how to rejoice, and surrounded as they ever were with death and disaster, each new day, as each new triumph, was indeed a cause for rejoicing.

"Men of victory!" Zan called above their din. "Remember the vow of friendship we have taken. No man may choose a wife within his own clan. This will be the path to our everlasting unity. I myself have promised to wed the granddaughter of Aniah with the permission of her family, whenever they think the time is ripe. And now, to ratify our unity, let us choose a single name for our people. We will no longer be this clan of the north or that of the south. Let us rename ourselves!" Aniah then proposed that the newly unified people should call themselves the Ba-Coro, the People of the Sling. The new name was received with loud and universal acclamation.

The noble celebration was not complete without a ceremony of union, much like an actual marriage of the clans. It was a formal ritual and a holy one, taking shape at night under the glare of smoking torches. Siraka-Finaka and the women of Ba-Coro took charge of this activity, for it was within their provence. Pairs of the women arranged themselves in a long double row, each facing her partner and taking her shoulders in an arch to form a human tunnel. Then, with great solemnity and primitive chant, the males of every clan crawled through the female passage on hands and knees while the women struggled and churned as if in the throes of childbirth. This turbulent activity signified the birth and kinship of a great new clan, and a willing submission to it. The men now did as the *women* directed. After all had emerged from the human tunnel, they deeply intoned their most sacred hymn to the spirits of earth and sky:

> *When the Sky took Earth as wife*
>
> *Giving love and giving life,*
>
> *She gave birth unto our race,*
>
> *Human virtue, human grace.*

14 THE HEALER

Dael had chosen to live. For a moment, when he crossed the great chasm, he had almost made up his mind to end his tormented life. Then the anxious face of Lissa-Na had told him her secret. She loved him—and needed him. How unworthy of that love he felt himself to be! He would have to stay alive for her, for Zan and the family, and go on enduring the devil phantoms that haunted and afflicted him. Afterwards, in the battle with the wasp men, he had succumbed for a time to his inward darkness and sought out the same death-wound he was dealing to his enemies. But again something within prevailed on him to go on living.

In the celebration of victory, the people rejoiced at his return, and made much of him. No man or woman but wished him well and said so. He ate and drank with them, and seemed to regain some of his energy and spirits. But at night he was visited by ghastly dreams which caused beads of sweat to stand out on his face. He was often seen gazing at the fire, his forehead twitching at some painful memory. More than once, in his blackest moods, he could be observed frowning darkly, as if deeply pondering some cruel revenge. Whole days went by without his saying a single word. He never laughed or joked as in former days. Never!

Lissa the Healer understood more than most. She knew that just as there are wounds of the body, there are wounds of the soul, and that both might leave awful scars. The claw marks of Zan-Gah were visible and he was proud to show them. They gave him no pain. Dael's hurts were not to be seen or shown, but they were deep, and might never entirely heal. Lissa knew that his life was torture to him, and she bent all her efforts to help and relieve him. Dael passed in time from despondency to a melancholy irritability. Everybody was patient and asked little of him—which irritated him the more. Lissa-Na endeavored in every possible way to comfort, to distract, to salve—while at the same time trying to make her efforts as little noticeable as possible.

After a year or two Dael seemed better and he began to take his place in the activities of his people, but he was still silent, morose, and short of patience. One evening, as the last of the orange sun was sinking under the horizon, his father, Thal, came to him and told him he should marry.

"Who?"

"Lissa-Na."

Dael paused. "Why not?"

Dael agreed to marriage without a word or thought, and Lissa accepted him as a homeless kitten that belongs to whoever takes it. Zan-Gah noticed with what indifference Dael received the young woman that meant so much to him, but he had long since realized that she was not to be his. With an effort he had put her from his mind and made other arrangements for himself. Zan's renouncement did not go unobserved by Lissa-Na, for she was not ignorant of his feelings, and she appreciated his silent sacrifice and love for Dael.

The council of elders made no objection to their union. In those remote days people married early, and often died young—frequently in childbirth. Zan-Gah, as he had promised, soon took Pax, the granddaughter of Aniah, for his wife. Aniah had long been as a second father to him and Zan felt honored to be his near relation. Although he had never ceased to admire Lissa-Na, he grew in time to deeply love his mate, albeit for different qualities. Chul and Aniah had already made their peace and eventually became good friends, even going hunting together. (And when are men more closely bonded than as fellow huntsmen?) All of the tribesmen took notice of the unlikely friendship of these former enemies, and it served as an example to them to forget old enmities.

Dael would heal in time, but he would not regain the glad disposition of his childhood. Many who knew him as a child wondered at the strange change that had taken place in him. It was for Lissa alone to penetrate a secret of great subtlety—that he who has been terribly hurt will often, and against all reason, blame himself. And that conception can shake and poison his inmost being. In her generous heart Lissa understood—and Dael was grateful that he would not have to relive those terrible days by speaking of them.

Dael's melancholy sickness was not to be quickly cured. Even married, his relationship with his wife long remained almost as patient and nurse. But the beautiful soul of Lissa-Na and the love of his family could not be denied forever. One day, in the spring of the year, Lissa announced to her husband that she was with child.

Dael smiled.

Warning: In his primitive world, Zan-Gah had to engage in a number of dangerous activities that should be avoided by the reader. Do not throw stones with a sling or use dangerous weapons, fish with your bare hands, taste unknown plants, climb or venture into dangerous places, nor hunt or attack animals, without the approval and supervision of your parents or a responsible adult.

Artist, teacher, actor, author, historian, and former Boy Scout, **ALLAN RICHARD SHICKMAN** was a professor of art history at the University of Northern Iowa for three decades. He now lives and writes in St. Louis.

IF YOU ENJOYED READING ZAN-GAH TELL YOUR FRIENDS!

ADDITIONAL COPIES MAY BE PURCHASED.

WEB ORDERS: www.earthshakerbooks.com

United States: $9.95   (Canada: $11.95)
Shipping & handling: $2 per copy (Canada $3)

MAIL ORDERS:

Please send me _____ copy(ies) of ZAN-GAH.
My check or money order payable to Earthshaker Books is enclosed.

Name _____

Address _____

City _____

State _____ Zip code _____

Country _____

Telephone _____

E-Mail address _____

AMOUNT ENCLOSED:

For Book(s) $ _____

For Shipping $ _____

Tax $ 0.73 $ _____
per copy (Missouri residents only)

Total $ _____

SEND TO: Earthshaker Books
P. O. Box 300184
St. Louis, MO 63130